T0118472

Haunted Horror

Ioannis Night

Order this book online at www.trafford.com
or email orders@trafford.com

Most Trafford titles are also available at major online book retailers.

© Copyright 2011 Ioannis Night.
All rights reserved. No part of this publication may be reproduced, stored in a retrieval system, or transmitted, in any form or by any means, electronic, mechanical, photocopying, recording, or otherwise, without the written prior permission of the author.

Printed in the United States of America.

ISBN: 978-1-4669-0756-0 (sc)
ISBN: 978-1-4669-0757-7 (hc)
ISBN: 978-1-4669-0755-3 (e)

Library of Congress Control Number: 2011962223

Trafford rev. 12/09/2011

 www.trafford.com

North America & international
toll-free: 1 888 232 4444 (USA & Canada)
phone: 250 383 6864 ♦ fax: 812 355 4082

Ω

It all started in England, in Oxford University neighborhood, around 4 o'clock in the morning during Summer time. That night had apparently nothing special, pretty dark and quiet, where not even a single sound could be heard and disturbed this completely silent night. As characteristic of a New Moon, that night was filled with a total darkness. The streets were only enlightened by lamp standards showing the way to the rare night pedestrians. It was just a mature night when all seemed to stop before Sun rises again. Suddenly, in this stillness peaceful environment, an intermittent sound broke the monotony of the night.

"Email email email". It was an electronic voice phenomena coming from a personal computer.

In that house, everyone was sleeping. But the voice had disturbed a boy's sleep. He started moving in the bed he shared with his girlfriend and accidently touched her.

"Hmmmm . . ." he starts waking up. The girl is still sleeping deeply without having perceived either the noise or her boyfriend who has just woken up.

The next second, the boy was out of his bed and walking towards the computer. It was completely dark but the blue light coming out from the computer's screen was enough for him to reach the desk located at the corner of the bedroom. Still blinded by the light, with his eyes half opened, he tried to check his email box. The light was still too bright for him and he found it hard to keep his eyes opened trying to read what was on the screen. And then he saw something strange. While his eyes were still trying to stay opened, he was trying to understand what he was reading on his e-mails. The light is too bright and he finds it hard to keep his eyes open watching at the same time on the screen. He had received an e-mail from a person whose name was unknown. It was a dark mail folder, instead of the normal white one, with a really strange sound as a background. It was like someone was singing a hymn. But it wasn't only one person's voice, but many!

"What the heck is this" he said.

He tried to open his eyes so as to see better, whipping them with his hand. He opens the e-mail and inside, the following message was written.

"Dear Zik

You probably don't know about me, but I know everything about you. I will pass this to you because you are the person that I believe that needs it the most. I have a mansion in southwest England and it's your heritance now. Details about the mansion and how to get there, can be found in the following pdf file"

Zik took his time to realize what was happening. He read the mail again and tried to open the pdf file. He was confused with the mail which he had just received out of nowhere but he wanted to read more about this unprecedented offer. So he did to open the pdf file.

"Ahhhhhh" an echoing and daunting voice came out of the pdf file making Zik fall behind.

"Really . . . what is that?" he asked himself.

He continued the reading of the document, but he wasn't so sure about the content of the file. He was the owner of a mansion now as it was written inside on the pdf file. He couldn't believe his eyes and the surprise on his face was easy to tell. Inside there were all the details and the ownership title and also directions of how to get there. He left the computer straight away and went back to his bed. With a smooth and gentle touch, he touched the left arm of his girlfriend.

"Angelina. My heart. Wake up. I have something to show you"

"Mmm . . . what happened? Why you are waking me up in the middle of the night Zik?" She said while trying to protect her eyes from the computer light, turning her head to the opposite side of the light.

"You should better come and watch this Angelina . . ." He said and walked back at the computer. She exhaled but she slowly, woke up from her bed and followed Zik to the computer. He showed her exactly what he had seen. The daunting sound was still there and creep Angelina too.

"Is this a scare maze or something? I am not in the mood for pranks." She said tired.

"No. It's a mail that I have just received. What do you think about this? "Zik asked her.

"I don't know what to tell you." she had a quick look at the mail.

"Ok, I am still sleeping and I can't give my full attention on this. Can we wait until the morning? I'll have more energy and ill understand it better. Now I don't even see what is written inside honey" she answered.

Zik scratched his head. And with a questioned face he said.

"Ok. Sorry that I woke you up anyway. Is just that it says something about me being owner of a mansion in a village and I was overexcited, since that it would be really beneficial for the both of us something like this to be true."

Angelina looked at him and said.

"Really? It says something like this? Hm . . . Maybe I'll have a better look now."

She saw the main theme of the e-mail and wondered why its appearance was so differently than the normal e-mails. She opened the folder and then the same echoing sound sounded. A sound like someone was whispering a hymn. She had more or less the same reaction that her boyfriend Zik also had when he opened it and she looked at him with a face full of query and agony of what was going on with that. At any rate, Zik pushed her to continue the reading of the subject in the e-mail, and by the time she had finished he asked her.

"So? What do you think?"

"I don't really know what to tell you. Maybe it's a prank. With all that scary background, you know. I have no idea. What about waiting until tomorrow and take it to someone that I know. Maybe he can provide us some short of help. We can figure out if it's real or not tomorrow right?"

"Ok. Let's go back to bed then. I'm still tired" he told to her and smiled at her giving her a goodnight kiss on her lips.

They both started walking back to bed. Then Zik stopped and went back to the computer to turn it off. He pressed the button and . . . tsffff. The sound of the deactivation sounded and the computer has been switched off.

Ω

The following morning, it was a murky weather. The sun was hidden and you could tell with a glance that it could rain. It was Wednesday morning of a hot Julie month. Although it was gloomy, the air it was warm. That morning found the young couple on an office. Zik was sitting on an armchair. He was around normal size tall, with brown hairs as well as well eyes. He was wearing a blue short pant and a green t-shirt and sandals on his feet. He had a nice body and he was a charming person. Next to him was sitting Angelina. She was blonde with blue eyes; someone could easily say that she looked like a princess because of her appearance. She was wearing a blue dress that its length was slightly above her knees and she was wearing a blue jean under that. She was also wearing sandals and she had her long hairs caught high plait all together with blue elastic. Both were around 23 years old. Angelina was sitting on an armchair too, next to Zik. In front of them was an old fashioned desk with a computer on the top and some papers. Behind that desk, an old man was sitting in a terrible old chair. The old man was wearing glasses and he had a serious face with lots of wrinkles, brown shoes and a brown pant with black shirt and his eyes were examining the computer screen. It was a small office with grey walls. It was quite until the man decided to break that silence.

"Everything seems true" he said with a serious look on his face and his voice had sounded like he was about to die.

"That means that the mansion it does exist and I own it?" Zik asked him with query.

"Well . . . you had of course to go until there and note it yourself. I am just telling you what the e-mail says. I personally believe that this is no prank. Although one thing concerns me" the old man said.

"What is that?" both asked at the same time.

"I can't find where the email came from. You have notice it as well I believe but it doesn't make sense. Why someone to send an ownership e-mail and not reveal his identity? Although I don't believe that it's a prank because it has lots of information's inside as well as serious law protocols, I would suggest you to not be that much of excited about this one, just in case"

And he continued saying.

"One last thing before you leave. How can someone insert in an e-mail those hymns and those shadows as a background?"

"Shadows? What shadows are you talking about Sir? I heard about the weird noise . . . hymn . . . whatever that was, last night, but apart from that, I didn't notice anything weirder than that. Like shadows for example!" Zik answered and he looked really amazed.

"When I opened the e-mail this morning, after you have sent it to me and come here, there were shadows of persons behind as a background.I thought that it was my computer and I restart it, but the e-mail had that shadow again. Come and have a look if you want" And he turned the computer screen at them, showing them the e-mail. Behind the letters you could discern lots of shadows, and the creepiest was that, they seemed like moving. Zik had a closer look and suddenly he saw it! He saw one shadow looking on his way, and suddenly everything disappeared! All the shadows have gone along with the hymns. It was only the dark background now.

"That was creepy . . ." he mumbled.

"The shadows are not there anymore! They have disappeared!"

Angelina was looking at the computer screen and didn't know if what she had just seen was real or not. She was wondering what was all that about and who could have possible send that e-mail in the first place. Someone who wanted to scare them or it was another internet virus?

"Did you see that? It looked at me. Even without eyes I know that that thing looked at me!" Zik agitated said to Angelina.

"I think that I saw it moved but I'm not sure. The only sure thing is that this e-mail is scary and really odd one. I still can't believe that someone out of nowhere gives you the rights to own utterly his house. And what that place, Haurr, never heard of it!"

she was getting more and more suspicious whether it was true or not.

"Sure. But that's why there is the map. You can't possible know all the small villages of the country. It says that is near that town, and has all the information's of how to go there." Zik told to Angelina, making a point against her worries.

"Well, maybe it's something wrong with the e-mail. Since you can't see who send it, maybe something went wrong from the beginning. But you don't lose anything if you go and take a look around there. I guess, in the worst scenario, you could have a summer trip. Isn't half bad having a trip this time of the year my boy." the old man said in order to make them feel better.

They looked each other, Zik and Angelina wondering what they should do. The e-mail was sure a scary e-mail, but they were thinking that it was just a mistake of the computer or something likewise. All those shadows and hymns maybe where part of a virus and that they should at least go there and check it out. They left the small office and before they do anything; they decided that they should not go alone in this trip. So they send a message to their best friends and asked them if they would like to join them and they were explaining them the whole situation and what they were thinking. They also said to them that in case the mansion doesn't exist, having a trip all together would be a good opportunity for them to have some fun.

During the next hours of the day, they had positive answers from all six of them. So they arranged to meet up in two days, on the university campus that they were attending classes during the season.

Ω

The morning after the next day, it was luminous. There were no more than two clouds on the clear sky. An enormous university building was standing behind a red jeep and a two seats black sport car, that were parked in the front parking of the university. Then, from inside the sport car a black boy came out. He didn't have the high of a basketball player but he was tall. He had brown eyes and short shaved hairs. He was wearing a black long sport pant and a black t-shirt with his nickname "Tiger" written on it. He was wearing White snickers and also wearing sun glasses. He had a well-trained body. He closed the door of the car and at the same time the other door from the left opened and a girl came out. She was a black girl, with long hairs and brown eyes as well as the black boy. She was wearing a blue short skirt and a black t-shirt. She was wearing white snickers and she had a well-trained body also. She closed the door behind her and covered her eyes with her right hand to protect her eyes from the sun. Tiger looked at the jeep that was parked opposite of them and said to the person sitting on the drivers' seat.

"Mark, have you talked with Zik? Is he coming yet or not?"

"I talked to him five minutes ago. He said that he was on the way. Besides, he doesn't live far. He is coming with the motorbike, so I suppose he will be here in something like two minutes. But, use your brain a little bit. He is always late in the class, why to change it now and come on his time" Mark answered back.

Mark was a tall man, something more than six feet and he was wearing classes. He had that nerd face and style but he had also an attitude in his face like "I know everything". He didn't have a well-trained body and he was holding a bag in his hand, with a map and several items to use for the jaunt.

Inside the car, in the seat next to Mark was another girl. Her name was Kathrin and she was Marks girlfriend. She looked also like a geek and she was wearing glasses too. Brown it was both favorite color and you could easily suspect it by seeing their clothes. In contrary to Angelina who she was blonde and Aprilia who was black, she was brunet and she had beautiful green eyes. Apart from that, she wasn't the most attractive girl among them. In the back seats, Stefan with his girlfriend Melody were sitting, along with their guitars. Stefan had all the time a set headphone on his ears and most of the time he was listening to rock music. Melody was holding Stefan's hand and she was happy that she had her boyfriend there. She was a shy person and she never liked to be in the spotlight. So she was just being quiet most of the time to keep a low profile and only with Stefan she was feeling safe.

"Mark! Were the hell is Zik? Its already 11 o clock and he is nowhere to be found! Is he coming??" Tiger asked again more impatiently.

"Gosh Tiger, can't you wait for some minutes?" Mark answered to Tiger and looked kind of pissed off cause of Tigers attitude. But it was always like this, they were having lots of arguments because they were different characters even thought they were in the same party.

"Do you want a piece of me four eyes? Because you know that I don't like your attitude at all, smartass!" Tiger told him and started walking to his direction when a sound of a motorbike stroked.

A big motorbike made especially for trips appeared with Zik and Angelina riding on it. The motorbike had three suitcases for travelling on it hanging from both sides of the motorbike and one was in the back. Zik stopped right in front of the cars, switched off the engine and took off his helmet. Angelina got off first and then followed Zik.

"Sorry for the delay but we had to take care of some stuffs before we leave the house. So, everyone is here. Shall we get going?" Zik proposed.

"It was about time man. I couldn't wait any longer. You know I don't like to wait for no one and nothing!" Tiger said pointing his finger on him.

"He already apologized, dumb ass." Mark said to Tiger and went into the car. Tiger did to hit him but he stopped it since he didn't want to lose any more of his precious time.

"Everyone follow me. I have searched in the internet and I found how to go there. I found the name of another village which is including on the direction that I have. So we go there first and we can ask. It's not far from this village, as it says in the instructions that were on the pdf file." Zik said.

The two cars and the motorbike had them engines switched on and the jaunt began.

The trip started at twenty past eleven in the morning. They have expected to be at the village near to Haurr in a couple of hours, but by hook, they lost their way and they did a circle around other villages. Being lost, they had a stop to one of those villages to get some rest, since they weren't in that much of a hurry, and to ask for information. They had lunch all together in a restaurant and having fun, the time passed. They found how to get to the other village but when they arrived there, it was already 6 o 'clock in the evening.

The village had lots of houses and it was foul of life. People were on the streets, children were playing around. It was a beautiful and peaceful village. The color of the sky was orange and it was a lovely evening to do lots of things, not to mention perfect, for a jaunt. They parked the vehicles outside of a cafe restaurant and Mark willed to go inside and ask for further instructions about their trip. His girlfriend Kathrin went with him, just to be sure that he wasn't going to do any mistake. Zik and Angelina get off the motorbike and went near Tigers car to chat, while waiting for Mark and Kathrin to come out.

Inside the restaurant there was at maximum ten people, two couples of old people, a drunken man who was sitting on the corner of the bar and three friends that they were chatting and having dinner most probably. Mark stepped inside and Kathrin followed right behind him. They both went to the waitress, who she was behind the bar, to ask about information of how to go to Haurr from there. She had a blue uniform, set, and a white apron. She was aged, something between fifty five and sixty.

Mark had always that tone, like he knew everything. He knew lots of things indeed but rather than that he had a big idea about himself. He wasn't muscle strong but that never prevented him from challenging stronger, muscled opponents and only by the power of speech, he was beating them. That's why he had offered to go inside the restaurant and ask for information's, since he was the most verbally skilled among them. Kathrin just followed him because she is like Mark. She likes to have the upper hand always and she wants to look strong when people are around. Having a boyfriend like Mark, making her looked stronger and she liked the way that Mark encountered situations and people. She was a smart girl but she knew that Mark was smarter and as a boy tougher than her, she was never picking up fights with him even if he was wrong sometimes. She liked what she had and she knew that one day Mark would be someone really important and she was waiting to have that power of his by her side. Mark from the other hand, liked Kathrin because she was smart and she was never talking back at him. He believed that she was the kind of the girl that had the man as a crown on her head and he liked that.

"Good evening" Mark said to the aged waitress. She looked at him with passivity.

"We would like to go to a village named Haurr and we are lost. Under no account we could find it on the map but we certainly know that is not far from here. So Madam, would you please provide us with some help?"

The old waitress was looking at him like she did not have understood what he was talking about. Mark looked back at her and he was expecting for an answer, but nothing came out from her mouth. She though for some minutes and then she answered.

"I do not know what you are talking about boy. That's the first time I hear that name. There is no such a village as Haurr around here. I can guaranty that. I am living here all my life."

"That cannot be . . . A friend of mine received an e-mail and it was written that if we wanted to go to Haurr, we should come here. It included this village's name. I am entirely certain. I read it twice before I come here. Before we all come here!"

"I don't think that I can help you." She said and turned her back at them. When she turned, something unbelievable happened. The atmosphere changed and the entire place was drawn into darkness. The waitress and Mark with Kathrin were the only ones visible. Everything else had disappeared. Mark fixed his glasses on his face and start looking around, amazed from what was happening. Kathrin on the other hand, was shocked since this was out of the ordinary. The old lady stood for a second with her back turned on them and suddenly she appeared in front of Mark's face looking at him into his eyes! She did not have the same skin color. She was whiter than before and more rotten and her eyes had no color. They were like two holes had taken the place of her eyes. That made Mark moved back two steps and he was staring at her with awe. Inside all this chaos that had happened, no one was saying a word. All happened so fast and they did not have a chance to react. They were just staying still and surprised. The dark scene was all over the restaurant and no one was able to see anything else than the faces of those three. The old waitress, the new dead looking old waitress, opened her mouth and dark smoke came out of it. It almost touched Mark. Even the thought of that thing touching him creep him out. He moved further back and caught Kathrin's hand that she could do nothing except staring with fear and surprise. After the dark smoke dissolved, the waitress spoke.

"You cannot find Haurr. Haurr will find YOU! Your lives are over now!"

Ω

As it had all turned dark, with the same way, it all turned as it used to be before. A regular restaurant and the waitress was the normal, not so friendly old woman, having her back turned at them again. Kathrin still unable to say anything and Mark looked as if he was totally lost. He went to the waitress who had her back turned on them and she was looking at the ordering stickers and touched her shoulder.

"Excuse me madam, but what was all this about? What have happened just now?" Mark asked her.

She looked at him and a bit annoyed, said.

"I do not know where that place Haurr is boy. What else do you want to know? It's the first time I hear that name! Go annoy somebody else. I am working right now! If you do not want to order something, stop annoying me! And she turned her back again on him, continuing doing her job. Mark did not like the way she threatened him and he wanted to ask more but he saw that Kathrin was shocked, so he decided to do not continue any further that pointless fight.

"Does anyone knows where Haurr is and how can we go there?" The people sitting inside the restaurant gave him a look but no one answered back and after some seconds, they continued doing their things. Mark grabbed Kathrin from the hand and dragged her outside. The others were talking and once Mark and Kathrin came out, they were waiting for them to tell them the route.

"I am sorry fellows. We asked and we got zero response. No one knew where Haurr is."

"Mark . . . Can I talk to you for a second?" Kathrin said.

She took him and went some meters away so no one could hear their conversation.

"What is it dear?"

"Mark! What was that inside the restaurant? I know that you saw what I saw!"

"I don't know what you are talking about." Mark said and looked away.

"You know exactly what I am talking about! What shall we tell them? I am scared! Something is wrong here!"

"We do not have anything to tell them! Maybe we were both dizzy from the trip and we had some sort of illusion. That explains why only I and you saw all that!"

"I am not so sure . . . I . . ." she trembled.

"Enough! Nothing happened. We are scientist and nothing happened and that's that!" He said and he went back to the others. Kathrin was still shocked and scared but she couldn't do otherwise and she was afraid that her friends will call her crazy if she was saying something nuts. So she just went back and she was kind of pissed off cause of Marks reaction.

Mark returned to them and tried to explain them that he could not take any information about Haurr, since no one inside the restaurant had ever heard of it. Kathrin was standing behind him without talking. They started thinking of how to go to Haurr and if they should ask somebody else. That time Kathrin raised a question.

"Zik! Did you notice anything weird or unusual when you received the e-mail?"

"Erm . . . Like what?" he said pretending that he did not know but he knew very well what she was talking about.

"I do not know . . . things out of the ordinary for example." Kathrin insisted.

"Well. Maybe there was something that I should have told you, but I found it a bit silly mentioning it so I just forgot about it."

"What was it?" Kathrin asked nervously.

"Something was strange about the e-mail." And so he started saying the entire story and how they ended up doing this trip. Everyone was listening except Stefan who was listening to his music. Once the story ended, Tiger said.

"And so what? I do not believe in ghost stories or supernatural phenomena."

"Something unusual happened inside the restaurant!" Kathrin said and looked at Mark who gave her a heated look.

"What exactly had happened?" Angelina asked her.

"The entire room become dark and the waitress inside, was like a dead person. She told us that Haurr will find us and . . ."

"Enough!" Mark broke her off.

"All those things are stupid. Most probably Zik, either you want to scare us or someone is making a prank on you!"

"A prank? Like A TV show you mean?" Zik said.

"I don't know. Maybe, but do not tell me that you can actually believe in ghost phenomena. This is stupid! I am at the physics department as well as you are Kathrin and more than anybody else here, you should not believe in those craps!" Mark said in words.

Tiger was observing the whole conversation with a serious face and Aprilia was holding his arm. In the meanwhile, Stefan the whole time was listening to music and had heard nothing about what was going on. Aprilia witnessing this, she decided to take the floor.

"Let us all calm down a bit here for a second. Me and Tiger, do not believe in ghosts anyway. We can consider the possibility of someone making a prank on us or especially, on you Zik, but even so, we have to go and find that village! We cannot stay here all day, let alone that soon is going to be dark. We will need a place to rest or to camp. Don't you all agree?"

They were planning in case that the e-mail wasn't real, to have a camp in any place available for doing camping and to have fun with their jaunt in any case. Aprilia was a good character. Honest and aggressive when need be. She liked to have strong persons by her side, not because she wasn't strong enough to protect herself but because she wanted to have someone as strong as she was. That's why she was with tiger. Both were athletic types and sharing the same goal. Be owners of a sport club or a gym. Tiger, liked strong women and with passion, a reason why he was with Aprilia. He liked her passion about sports and her hot temperament. But more than that, he liked a good looking athletic body to his girlfriend. So Aprilia was the perfect partner for him. Tiger was a silent type. Concentrate only to his studies and his trainings. He wanted to win for once more the national champion title on the heavy boxing category. He was a strong man knowing no fear. He didn't like to wait for anyone or anything and he didn't have a problem to start a fight with no one and nothing.

"I will go and find someone to tell me how the hell to go to that village or we can go NOW and search it ourselves!!!!" Tiger said filled with anger. He was already waiting for a long time and he could not bear it any longer.

"Ok. I suppose that we can find it. I mean, with luck we can find it." Zik said.

"Don't fear the reaper . . . baby take my hand . . . don't fear the reaper" Stefan started singing quietly and even if his eyes were directed on the others, he had no sense at all.

"I don't believe you Stefan. Are you for real?" Kathrin said and she moved negatively her head. But Stefan did not respond at all. He continued listening to his music.

"Forget about Stefan. It's high time we left! We are going to find it at any rate. We don't need directions." Tiger said and started walking impatiently back to his car. He suggested on Aprilia to follow him and so she did. He ignited the engine and he was waiting for the others to follow his example. Zik and Angelina got on the motorbike and the rest of them went into Marks car. Kathrin was still thinking about everything she had seen. She did not know what to believe and Mark who saw that she was not alright, tried to explain her that all that was probably a prank and nothing more. The vehicles started moving again and went out of that village. They were blinding following Tiger. No more than fifteen minutes had passed and suddenly something abnormal happened. The all good clean orange sky was becoming darker and darker. But that was not the abnormal thing since it was about to get dark because of the time. Abnormal was the fact that the wind had started to become really strong and the sky it looked like it was about to rain! They did not know where they were heading and all that bad weather was not helping them at all. It was a total climate change.

"This is unexpected. I thought that we were going to have a nice weather. Not rains and wind like we use to have on winder. Not this early at least." Zik thought and continued following

Tiger who was leading. Few kilometers later, Zik overtook Tiger and he was in front of them now, him leading the way.

The sudden amend of the weather wasn't the only surprise. While they were driving, they saw from afar, a gate, similar to ones that people used to build some years ago, when someone was entering on a village. The entrance was consistent by two big iron pillars, one on the left and one on the right side of the road and above those pillars; an old sign with the word Haurr written on it. It had some other letters as well but they couldn't read them because the time had made them too turbid. First thing that you could see in the village, were trees and only trees in order. They were one after another, big imposing trees with dark shadows around them. Those trees had no leaves and they were giving a creepy feeling. The sky was really dark but you could see everything cause of the moonlight. There were no traffic lights or any light, since the road did not exist in the map. So they believed that no one really was carrying about some forgotten village and that is why there were no lights around. Believe it or not, they were at Haurr and it was already night. The wind it was wild and you could hear the sound of it. As they were driving, Tiger speed up and his sport car started to increase that much speed, that the others couldn't reach them easily and overtook Zik. In the end of the street, the road was splitting. One side was leading to the left and the other side was leading to the right. Tiger drove to the left way and suddenly they all saw something horrifying. A dark mist appeared out of nowhere and with no vision, the others couldn't follow him. Zik made signal to Mark to stop and both stopped before the splitting part of the road. Zik went off his motorbike and went until Marks car. He knocked the window and Mark opened it.

"Man. What is that in front of us? With that mist you cannot see anything! It came out of the blue!"

"Do not be afraid my friend. We will take the other path and since we are already in the village, we will meet them for sure later somewhere!"

"I hope so. Why he speed up in a first place anyway" he sigh.

"Forget about it. We will follow the other road and if we don't find the village we will return here. Do you agree?"

"Ok, I agree!"

"Am I the only one that is scared by all this?" Kathrin said.

"What do you mean?" Zik asked her.

"Come on guys! Something is wrong with this trip since the beginning!!!"

"Don't you think this as a prank from a TV show or something alike?" Zik asked Kathrin and at the same time looked at Mark.

"YES IT IS!" Mark said and looked Kathrin mad. She said nothing more and sank deep into her seat looking at Mark.

Zik returned to his motorbike and he started driving, him leading the way again, while Mark was following him. They drove for less than five minutes and the village showed up. The first house came out up and then another one and another. There were Houses in both sides of the street. Nicely architectonically build. Between the houses were some stores. A tailor's workshop, butchery shops a bookstore and so on. Even if you could see the village, you couldn't see anyone, like the village was abandoned. The houses were in a good condition as well as the shops, but there was no one living . . . This village it was nicely build, like all the residents, had agreed to build it in an order. Everything was in line and there was not space for something new. It was like the village was perfect as it had!

"Zik, do you have the address?" Angelina asked him while they were on the motorbike.

"Yes, I have it. But isn't it too quite here? Or is it just my idea?"

"Yes it is. It feels like no one is here, but I guess that in small villages like this one, people has the notion ongoing to bed early. Furthermore, do you see any address on the streets? How we will go to the one that we have?"

"Actually the address says "Hill" and then it says "Haurr Mansion". Also says easy to be found, as I see here."

Ω

They keep driving inside the hollow city and Zik was driving slowly so as to not lose the mansion in case he was passing in front of it. Mark was following him fixed. There were few stores, about twenty houses beside each street and the main square with the Town Hall and opposite of it was laying the library. Both the library and the Town hall were huge buildings! They had only a quick look on the village and in the next corner after the main square there was a long road that it was straight directed to the mansion. Zik saw the mansion and gladly show it to Angelina.

"That is Amazing!" Angelina said.

"I can't believe in my eyes that this is the house" Zik told her and they both looked amazed.

The motorbike stopped in front of a huge iron gate. Mark, who was following them, stopped the car too.

"Tell me that this is the place?!" Mark said.

"I think so my friend" Zik said to Mark.

"I don't believe that this is a prank at all. Look at that Mansion. It looks like the ones that we see on horror movies with haunted houses!" Kathrin said inside the car.

"That is why I'm more certain now, that this is a prank!" Mark gladly said.

"It does not even pass through your minds that maybe nothing is going on and the mansion does really belong to me? Zik said frustrated.

"I am sure that this is a well-made studio and if not, then they are using it for their purpose to scare us. Try to relax Kathrin and Zik. My friend, If you are so lucky to own this one over here, then, congratulations!" and Mark kissed Kathrin on the chick in an attempt to calm her down and made her feel better.

They continued until the main gate of the mansion. It was a large iron cage gate. Zik pushed the door and opened it. The mansion was a hundred meters or less from the main gate but in the meanwhile there was nothing but dry ground. The gate opened easily and no key required. The ground smelled like rain and the appearance was not nice. The mansion it was enormous from the outside. It was a huge building with lots of windows and you had to make a round to a big alley in order to see it all. There was one door only as they could see and they went to this door. They switched off the engines and they debarked from their vehicles. They were approaching the door. Mark did to see inside the mansion from the window but the curtains were blocking his view. Zik tried to open the door by pushing it with his hand but it was locked!

"Great . . . and now how am I supposed to unlock it?" he wandered and looked around.

Kathrin was holding hands with Mark but still she was looking around terrifying. She really didn't want to be there.

Angelina started looking around for the key and wondering where it could possibly be. Stefan was on his own world. Still listening to music and Melody was just waiting holding Stefan's hand. The atmosphere was spooky. There was only the light coming from the moon in that area but at least the wind had calmed down and it was warm again. Suddenly the door opened by itself. The six juveniles looked at the door that was opening by itself with surprise.

"Ha! Now I'm completely sure that this is a TV show and they want to scare us and to fall into their little trap!" Mark said and made the first step inside leaving Kathrin behind.

"This isn't going to work with me fellows!" he shouted inside the mansion and smiled.

"Awesome! Stefan said and he moved his head with pleasure.

"Let's all go inside and try to find the switches for lights!" Zik said enthusiastic and he stepped inside too. Then the lights turned on.

"Maybe someone activates them like before or maybe the whole mansion has a new voice activating system" he also said.

"Am I the only one that does not want to go inside a house that opens by itself lights and doors? Does this seem normal to you!???" Kathrin started telling them off!

"OH!! Come on Kathrin! You don't get it? You still believe that this is a haunted mansion? IT IS A PRANK!" Mark said out loud.

"OK. And hypothetically that someone is watching as and wants us to be scared. Where is Tiger and Aprilia? Are they a part of this prank too, or they just gone MISSING!!!???" she was pissed off obliviously but more than that they knew that she was too scared.

"That's right! Tiger is behind it as well! I am sure that he did not like the idea of being scared so he made a deal with the producer, or he was a part on this prank since the very beginning! Mark said proudly.

So he said and crabbed Kathrin from her hand and made her step inside. The mansion it was in a really good condition and you could easily say that it was a newly build one.

Ω

Lying in front of their eyes was this picturesque living room. Bloody red velvet curtains were framing the windows, and all the furniture seem to belong to another past century. It was all impressive and magnificent. A couple of long sofas in one side of the room were accompanied by a fireplace and spiral staircase was showing the way to the top floor. Large crystal chandeliers were hanging on the ceiling. On the other side of the room, there was the entrance to the kitchen.

There was the kitchen, next to the living room. It was a huge kitchen fully equipped with all kitchenware imaginable. Going through the kitchen, there was a closed door.

All the space from the living room to the kitchen were well optimized and amazingly decorated. The floor was all in marble covered partly with ancient carpets. It was at least two hundred square meters all together.

Following a quick look inside the kitchen, Mark tried to open the other door but realized that it was locked. Therefore they decided to go to the upper floor to continue their visit. It was before they heard a sound, a sound like when you lock a door.

"What was that?!" Kathrin said out loud.

"Don't ask me!" Zik said. He then ran toward the door and when he tried to open it, his thoughts seemed to be unfortunately true. It was locked. He kept trying twisting the handle harder but even with both hand he could not get to open it.

"Come on! How did that happen?" he yelled!

"Come on guys. Relax! They are trying to scare us. Remember!?" Mark said with a serene voice.

"That CALMNESS of yours starts DRIVING ME CRAZY MARK!!!" Kathrin screamed at him.

"Can you please relax?" Mark said to Kathrin fixing up his glasses on his noise.

"You are too scared and it's stupid. Try to stay cool. There is no such a thing as ghosts around here or anything like. Take Stephan as an example. He is so calm!", showing Stefan who had not said a word yet and still smiling enjoying his music.

"I suggest that we call up Tiger to figure out where he is and move our luggage to our rooms. Then we will figure out what to do. Ok?" Mark commanded.

"I don't really mind about the door. My concern is that someone can lock us inside at any time." Zik mentioned.

"Whatever . . . I hope that you are right with all these TV show theories!" and Kathrin who was obviously pissed off, went upstairs.

"Is she going to be alright? She seems too angry with you all?" Melody said.

""She is scared, Melody. That's all. Let's go upstairs" Angelina interrupted and all of them started following Kathrin.

Upstairs, there was a long corridor with lots of doors. A red carpet covered the floor and there were the same chandeliers as in the living room above their heads lighting the way. In the end of it, there was a Crystal door. Melody headed that way and stopped in front of it. The others followed her to see what that door was too. It was a really wonderful but riddling door.

"That one is really nice" Melody said while touching it with her hand.

"What is it behind it?" Mark said and he tried to open that door but again in vain.

"It's locked. I'm sorry Melody but it seems that you will have to wait to see what's inside." He said and started to moving back to the other doors.

"It is kind of funny that every door Mark is trying to open is locked" Stefan said smiling. The others did not really pay attention on what he had just said and they headed back to the first doors that they have seen.

"Let's open the door one by one and see what is inside" Angelina suggested.

They opened the first door and it was a bedroom, just as normal as a bedroom could be. So they opened the other doors and they were all normal-type bedrooms, all until the end of the corridor. At the end of the corridor, the door would not open as it was locked. They tried to open it but they did not succeed, so they moved on and went back to the bedrooms.

Zik and Angelina took the first one. Next to them, moved in Mark with Kathrin and in the following bedroom Stefan and Melody started unpacking. Inside Zik's bedroom, there was a big old commode, with a large and old mirror. Everything in the house was from the last past century. A closet was standing opposite to the mirror, also looked ancient and valuable. The bed cover was out of silk. Red was the main color of this room with white walls which would capture all your attention. Everything, every detail in the room, was in harmony with the entire mansion. Above the bed, there was a golden plate with something engraved on it. It was dusty, so Angelina started cleaned it up with her fingers to read it. She read the inscription:

"Jessica and Lewis Anderson"

"What did you say?" Zik interjected as he was looking through the window and had not noticed what she had just say.

"It's written here, on the plate above the bed." She said. Zik turn his head at her and started looking at the golden plate. A bunch of questions started rising in his head. Who were that couple? Where are they now? Still looking around, he opened the only drawer of the commode. He discovered a book. He took it, and after having investigating it a bit he opened it at the first page and start reading it.

"This is the diary book of Lewis and Jessica Anderson but we are the owners of the Haurr mansion!"

"Why everything is so cleaned and tidy? Do you believe that this is really a prank sweetie?" Angelina asked Zik.

"I do not know. I hope that the mansion really belongs to us." She mumbled while reading the book.

The book had a leather hard cover of about 150 pages. It was manuscript and the last pages were blank. Zik just read quickly the first three pages and said to Angelina.

"It's something like a diary but it doesn't seem interesting, or important" then he put it back to the drawer and pushed it to close it.

"I'll read it later if you do not mind honey. I like diaries because they reveal little dirty secrets!" Angelina said smiling enthusiastically.

"Yeah sure, do as you like, if it's not fixed yet. I do not know what to believe anymore. Are any of these real? Or someone is just messing up with us?" Zik was worried as if it was a prank or not; after all he really wanted to own the mansion.

Meanwhile, a heavy noise came out of the next room where Mark and Kathrin had decided to stay.

"Oh Mark! What have you done! You destroyed the furniture! Don't you see that is an antiquity? Maybe it wasn't supposed to open."

"Is it my fault? I wanted to see what was inside the commode but the drawer seems stocked and accidently I broke it! I didn't mean to do it."

He had destroyed the furniture but he had managed to taken out of the drawer a book.

"This is the personal book of Zeta Cronty. First maid of the Haurr mansion"

"Na Na Na . . . Nonsense, nonsense, nonsense. It's an ill-advised diary. Who is going to read that? There is nothing special on it. I never in my life liked those books. I don't even understand why people write them in a first place. No knowledge can be acquired from them, so they are useless". He said and threw the book on the bed.

"Any other book than the scientific ones that you read, is just unworkable, with no interests at all, right Mark?!" Kathrin said annoyed.

"Not true. I like other books too, but this is nothing. I thought that I could find something more interesting than an old diary. But come to think of it. This prank is well made. They have done lots of preparations to scare us and make us believe that this is all real. I am starting to believe that the show is from someone really wealthy."

"Whatever." Kathrin shook her head negatively, because she didn't agree with Marks theory but she did not want to continue that conversation.

"Since that trip started, I don't like your attitude at all. All the stupidity you have come to the surface!"

They continued arguing when the door opened letting the other couples enter the room. Melody was holding a book similar to the other ones and Stefan was still listening music. Zik with Angelina followed too.

"We have found that book. It's the personal book of the housekeeper" Melody said and showed them a book exactly like the two others.

"You aren't the only one. We have one in our room too" Zik said.

"So, in this mansion, everyone had to write every day on a diary, or what?" Mark said hoaxing.

"We have started to believe that maybe this mansion is part of the prank too." Angelina added drily.

"Can be, but right now I'm a bit hungry. I suggest that we all should go downstairs and eat something. I hope that they have thought of the food and filled up the fridge otherwise I am ready to break the main door in order to find something to eat." Mark said and starting going toward the stairs.

They all went to the kitchen downstairs, after Mark suggestion. After all, they were rather hungry, had not eaten anything since lunch. Melody had the book in her hands and started reading it. The kitchen even though was in perfect condition and absolutely cleaned, had nothing edible and everyone was disappointed especially Mark that yelled angry!

"Ok. Come on now. We know that it is a prank but we are hungry here. Give us some food for God sake. Do I really have to break the main door and go outside to look for something?"

His voice resonated into the Mansion, but he got no answer.

"That is outrageous. I'm tired with their games. I was trying to be cool and everything but this is annoying. I'll find them and ill beat them, with your help Zik" he looked at him expecting for his alliance.

"I guess so. Let's go and find them. Girls, you stay here please and don't go anywhere. This is a big mansion and I don't want you to be lost. Stay here and Stefan will take care of you. We will be right back!" and they went to the locked door. They knew that it was locked but Zik tried one more time to open it just in case and really an echoed sound sounded when he turned the handle. The door has been unlocked and opened to another long corridor.

"Be careful!" Kathrin and Angelina said with concern.

They start walking but they couldn't see. Then Mark suggested to Zik that they should try speech recognition just in case. Zik agreed and after they yelled "Lights On" the lights switched on and the entire place illuminated!

"Nice. They are still going on with the prank . . . The annoying thing with them is that they always trying to make you mad but no scared. What kind of a prank is this one?" Mark said to Zik.

They moved on the corridor and the door closed suddenly behind them!

"Zik, Mark!!! Are you alright?" Angelina shouted.

"Not since I got here but forget it." Mark said through his teeth.

"We are alright but we can't unlock it. We will find whoever is behind this and we will tell him or them, to not go any longer with that prank. Maybe we will also find Tiger and Aprilia. So you don't need to worry! We will be back in no time. I love you sweetheart!" Zik answered nicely.

"Love you too darling!" Angelina voice sounded from the other side of the door.

They went back to the kitchen to wait for them until they come back. Melody was happy that she had Stefan with her but Kathrin was worrying about everything that was going on in the mansion. Now that they split up, her agony went greater than before. They could not hear anymore Zik's or Mark's steps. Angelina was anxious too but she was a strong person. She always knew how to protect herself and she had learnt lot from the life and how to survive. She knew what to do most of the times and to remain calm in every situation. She had lost her father when she was young and since then she had to fight on her own for almost everything in her life. She was with Zik because he was a man that would never give up and he would do everything in order to protect his beloved ones. So she was trying to remain calm and make the atmosphere lighter.

"Do you know something Mark? I think that I have already been here by the past."

"What do you mean?" Mark asked him suspicious.

"Or I was here when I was really young or maybe I dreamt about this place"

"OH . . . Good to know man." Mark said indifferently.

They were walking through the corridor. The red carpet was on this floor too and old paintings were on the walls. Zik stopped in front of one portray and started staring at it. That painting was the representation a little girl, running in an open air. A green hill filled with lots of flowers and multiple colors. She was a young girl with brown eyes and glossy brown hairs. The next one was depicting the same young girl crossing a shallow river barefooted, holding up her dress to do not get wet. She had a smile on her face enjoying the refreshing cold water. Then he moved to the third painting. This same girl was painted again with that same expression on her face. She seemed happy but it was like she had a dolly's face. Even though it was painted, her face was really strange and Zik pointed at it.

"Those portraying are creepy. Have a look Mark!" Mark did not respond. Zik gazed him and he saw him looking at the last painting of the corridor with fear on his face!

"What's wrong? Zik said and went prompt near him.

"What is that?!" Zik said with surprised on his voice when he witnessed the portraying. He got Goosebumps on his spine too.

They were looking at a portraying that was depicting the young girl having the same insane smile in her face and she was covered in blood inside the living room that they were before and all of their friends, including them, were lying dead on the floor. They could not believe in their eyes and while Mark was having a better look then the eyes of the girl

"IT MOVED!" Mark screamed and by doing backwards, he slipped and fell on the floor. Zik was glaring at the girls face and she was looking at Mark smiling. Smiling with that creepy smile, showing her teeth and look like an insane killer.

Ω

In the meantime inside the kitchen, Melody was reading the personal book of the house keeper with awe!

"Erm . . . I'm sorry . . ." she said shyly.

"What is it Melody?" Angelina asked her with kindness on her voice.

"I am reading something weird in this diary" added shyly.

"Tell us. What is it?" Kathrin said.

Angelina and Kathrin behold her and they were waiting to hear what she had to say. Stefan was continuing listening to his music, but abruptly he stopped. He took off his headphones and after having a quick glance at the kitchen, he said.

"That mansion is really nice. I am wondering if it has any secret passages like the one that we see in the movies on houses like this one" he said smiling.

"Is he always like that?" Kathrin asked Melody.

Stefan he was a cool person with no worries. He was studying music and he liked it a lot. In the auditorium met Melody and he liked the fact that she has shy. After he got to know her better, she became more as an easy going person, he started having feeling for her and they became a couple. Stefan was never taking off his headphones because that would take him out of this unconcerned world which he was wishing he could stay in for good.

"Whatsoever. Please tell us what is written inside the book. I am curious Melody!" Angelina said uncomfortably.

"Ok. I'll start reading it then." Melody began the reading with her soft, low voice.

"This is my personal book. My name is Adam Black. I am the housekeeper of the Haurr mansion. This very mansion . . . no better . . . this very village has a big secret. I am the only one who can write the truth of this town without consequences, for the reason that I am too old and I will die soon. No one cares about what I am doing. I hope that the people who will come here after us in case I do not make it, will be aware and it may also succeed when we will have failed! Every village has dark secrets but this one is the darkest of all. Those personal books, we are forced to write them by Lewis. I don't know why he wants it, but I am sure that has something to do with THAT. Because I don't really mind about writing it, I will never even bother to ask why. Maybe they want to keep an eye on us or to keep tracks of our daily events? I don't know. But I certainly know that. Whoever read this book, from now on, shall be aware that he has to leave this village immediately, if of course . . . what am I saying? . . . most probably you will not be able to leave . . . as all of us, you will be prisoner of THAT. I think that I spend already enough time thinking how should I write this. I am no good in writing after all. It's time to start again and this time I will get in the matter straight away. It's the first day that our boss told us that we have to write those personal books. It wasn't always like this. But something changed and I'm afraid it's because of me. Maybe it is afraid of me now that I know things . . . Only the people who lives in the mansion (the rest people in the village are just peasants and they don't matter), have to write them. My bosses' names are Jessica and Lewis and they are both possessed by THAT, even if I am not utterly sure about that! I don't know where it came from or how but it is here now. No one can leave the village; its powers are great and I think that we will all be soon as good as dead"

"That's the only thing that is written inside and that is why it made me want to show it to you. The rest pages are blank . . ."

"Maybe he died and he never got the chance to finish it." Angelina said making a supposition.

"Or someone or something stopped him. That is one more reason why we should act smart and leave the village straight away!" Kathrin said worried.

"Why you say that? You do not believe that all this is part of the prank?" Angelina said.

"I don't believe that it is a prank at all. Isn't it suspicious that he was ready to write something so important and suddenly the rest book is covered with blank pages?"

"I don't believe that is a prank too. I feel that there is someone watching us." Melody said and went closer to Stefan who was sitting on the table.

"Let's go all together upstairs and check the other books in each room. If this is a prank it is a really well made one! I had to confess that I started being frightened! Angelina said.

"Finally a little drop of support!" Kathrin happily added.

"I . . . I am with you girls!" Melody added too and Stefan put the earphones on his ears again and smiled.

All four went again upstairs and opened each one and every door in the rooms, searching for the personal books. In the end they had gathered them all. It was like twenty books in total, from every single person that was living in the rooms of the mansion, at least in this floor. The up floor had in total forty rooms. In one side there were the bedrooms and opposite of those there were the bathrooms. They tried to find similar books to the one Melody read, but they were all like diaries and nothing more. It was written only the daily life of each person, but they didn't search for more details since there were lots of books to get through and they didn't see anything as immortal as this on Adams book.

"Waste of time. And the boys are yet to be back. It's completely dark outside and I'm scared. Plus I haven't eaten anything all day and I am hungry. I should have eaten in one of the restaurants that we went!" Kathrin complained.

"That's right Kathrin!" Angelina said happy.

"What is right? That I should have eaten something?" Kathrin curiously said.

"Not about that but about the dark outside. You can see the sky, which means that we have windows and we didn't even try to escape using them!"

"True! I am wondering why we didn't think of trying it earlier. Of course Mark was obsessed finding out about the prank but anyway, it doesn't matter now!"

They were in the last room of the up floor which was next to the locked made by crystal door. They went near to the window and that moment they heard a voice. They all met their gaze, apart from Stefan, whose of course couldn't hear anything since he was lying on the bed and he had his earphones on. The voice it sounded like a young girl's voice but it wasn't clear enough so they to understand what she said.

"What was THAT?" Kathrin said and her voice filled with horror.

"I think it was like a girls voice coming out from the corridor." Angelina answered.

They went slowly outside of the room to check but there was no one there. On the other hand, the crystal door that once was locked now it was ajar. The three of them went closer to the door. Angelina pushed the door lightly to open it. The door opened without making any sound and a bright light appeared from that room. It was a bright room with millions of small lights on the roof and mirrors covering all the walls. The first thought which came into their minds was that of a dancing room! The lights and the mirrors were giving a bright and joyful emotion, nothing alike to their feelings of fear that they had some seconds ago. Over their heads, a crystal ball was hanging and on the floor in the center of the room, right after the ball, there was a red carpet. The three girls got captured by the dazzling light, and they did not notice that the door was closing unhurriedly behind them. The door gradually closed and only the sound of the locker made them realize that the door had closed and more than that, they were locked in now. Angelina rushed to the door and grabbed the knob. She tried to open it but didn't need more than a second to realize that this was never going to happen. She tried harder another two times, before she gave it up. Kathrin and Melody were waiting with agony. Angelina turned her back to the door and anxiously said.

"That door is locked again . . ."

"No!!! This cannot be happening! You mean that we are trapped in this room!?" Kathrin said and started searching around like a maniac to find another exit to escape. Her look met the two doors on the opposite side of that big dancing room. Then terror overwhelmed her. In one of the two doors, a young girl was standing and watching them. A young girl with a creepy smile had appeared in the room. She was just observing them, standing in front of the left of the two doors that were in the opposite side of the room.

"If you want you can try to open it. I can't do it Kathrin. It's locked." Angelina answered frustrated. She had begun getting weaker because she could not handle anymore all those weird things that were happening from the beginning of the jaunt. She was waiting for Kathrin to say something, but she didn't. So she turned her head back and saw her to looking on something terrified. Angelina turned her head more and looked where Kathrin was looking.

"Aaaaa!!!" she screamed. That was an instant reaction of what she was looking at. She could not take her eyes away too, from the little girl, with the so creepy and scary appearance.

"Who are you?" Angelina found the courage to ask.

The little girl did not answer. She did a step back and the door behind her opened by itself fast. The girl turned her back and started running into darkness. Angelina looked Kathrin whose she was socked. She caught her hand and tried to bring her back to her sense. Melody start asking what had happened and why Kathrin was acting like that. She hasn't seen anything because she was captured by the beautiful lights. Kathrin took a long breath and sat on the floor.

"There was a little girl who looked like a monster over there." Kathrin said and showed her the point.

"I don't know what to say. I am really scared too" Angelina added.

Stefan!!! Stefan!!! Can you hear me?" Melody started yelling with her soft voice as loud as she could and punching the crystal door. But the door was too thick for someone to be able to hear something from the other side. Being a dancing room, it had thick walls so as no sound to going out of this room all together.

"It's pointless Melody. That door is too thick plus that Stefan is wearing his headphones. The only option that we have is to go over that door on the left. Or the other one if it's unlocked.

Somehow they felt that, whatever they were doing, something was luring them somewhere without them having much of a choice. Cold air was coming from the opened door along with an unpleasant feeling. It was totally dark after the door and they could not see anything.

"Shall we go in there or not?" Angelina said without being sure if wise was.

Ω

Stefan back to the room was lying on the bed listening to music. He did not realize that the three girls, including his girlfriend had left the room. For some reasons, he woke up and opened his eyes. He had a look around and started wondering where they could be. He took his headphones off and started calling after Melody going out of the room. He shouted her name three times, and then he started calling the other girl's names as well. He got no answer so he went near to the crystal door. He tried to open it but, not surprisingly, it was locked so he did not insist any longer. He also was convinced that they could not have possible been behind the door.

He decided to go back to the room and wait for them to return. Then he remembered that last time he saw them was when they were all standing near the window. He thought that maybe they could have decided to leave the mansion through the window. Because the window was slightly opened, his suspicions became greater. He opened the window even more to have a look outside, but then it was hard for him to believe that they have jumped from that high. It was four or five meters high at least.

"They couldn't have jumped from that high." He said to himself.

He was shutting the window when something pushed him from behind making him going through it, He fell from four or 5 meters high but luckily enough, he felt on a soft ground and eased his fall. He ended up with only small scratches. While he was on the ground, he started getting up holding his back with one hand as to check if he was injured. After that, he stopped moving and lay down on the ground. Lying in the middle of the mud, smell of the moist soil that made him blinked a couple of times. The only thing he was worried of what his music player.

"I fell . . . I hope that I didn't break my mp4 player. The area around here smells like dead body. It's awful. He he!" He said laughing.

He stood up and he put his headphones back to his ears again. The player was still working. So he stood up and walked to the front entrance. The door was locked as he expected. He started checking at windows and a way to get in through one of them, but there were all locked from the inside therefore he could not get in from there either. He stood back and looked at the mansion. He was investigating it from the top to the bottom. It was a picturesque mansion. He wanted to see how big it was, so he started running around the mansion. It took him a long minute to complete the tour even though he was running fast. Back to the main entrance, he had one more look at the mansion and he said:

"It is a really big mansion and no ways to get inside apart from the front door. I could break the door or a window, but I don't think that it is appropriated. Well actually, Zik and Angelina will understand."

He decided to break to force the door. Joining his palms together, like a hero out of a comic book, he hit the door. Nothing happened. He continued doing some silly and nonsense things, like shouting out loud the names of his attacks and kicks. Predictably, he failed. Then he tried to break a window using his elbow. The glass broke in small pieces. For a second, he smiled but this smile quickly disappeared, when he assisted a weird thing. All the little pieces of glass, even before touching the ground, flew in the air and got back together fixing the window in one piece again. It looked brand new, like nothing had happened. Stefan was shocked and started wondering.

"What was that?" Through the window, he noticed something. A dark shape but a face materialized in it. The face turned to a fearful face screaming as it was approaching Stephan. Stefan tried to see better, he could not react to what he had just seen. The face eventually faded. All vanished and everything was normal again. Wondering what next to do, he said to himself:

"So . . . I can go to the town and search for Tiger. Now there is nothing better I can do. And to be honest, I would love to have a walk and see the village." he seemed happy with his decision and he went to the gate. He realized that someone had closed it. But he didn't even bother, because he could fit to pass through it. He continued his way to the town. There were lights on the streets all the way to the village but the weather was terrible. It was foggy to some extent and the wind was blowing so hard that he started getting annoyed. It was night time, even though it was summer, it was very chilly.

Ω

In the meanwhile inside the ball room, Angelina Melody and Kathrin were standing before the opened door. They could see nothing but darkness and that was making it harder to make a choice should they go in or not.

"Kathrin, do you mind try opening the other door?" Angelina pleased her.

"Be sure that I will. I prefer to try any other option than to go over there!" She walked from the one door to the other. The two doors were not close to each other, they had a five or six meters distance. She crabbed the doorknob. At first she thought for a second whether she should open it or not. Because she did not have any idea what could have been hidden behind it she was having doubts. Finally she took the choice to enter and much to her surprise, it was unlocked!

"Girls! It's unlocked!" She cheerfully yelled, and opened it. Instantaneously a black non-human hand appeared from inside the room, crabbed her and dragged her straightaway inside, locking the door behind it. Kathrin didn't even have the chance to scream. She only made a small screech before the door shut.

Then throughout the crystals, shadows appeared and were moving from mirror to mirror. The light started to faint away and it was becoming darker and darker inside the room. Even if it was dark, there was still enough light for them to be able to see the shadows. They were jumping and moving inside the crystals making a weird sound like scratching, on the crystals.

"What is going on?" Melody said scared watching above her!

"I don't know Mel. We have to go and help Kathrin before something happen to us too!" Angelina run and tried to open the door on the right. Whatever she tried, nothing happened. This door it was undoubtedly locked.

"I don't like this place!" Melody heavily breathing said and started crying.

"Shit! The only way out now is through that door." Meaning the one that had no lights.

"Go in there quickly Melody!" pushing her with the tone on her voice to hurry.

"Kathrin isn't with us. It's not nice to leave her alone in there. She could be in great danger and she may need our help!" Melody told Angelina crying.

"I am well aware of that. But right now we cannot do anything else. Let's go inside there because it's dangerous to stay here any longer." From the crystals, darkness had started coming out and the noises were becoming louder and louder. She run back again crabbed Melody's hand and went inside the room shutting the door behind them.

Ω

Mark was still lying on the floor after the sock he had earlier, having seen the anomalous painting. Zik went near him and helped him to stand up. Some minutes after the moving eyes incident, they both calmed down and they tried to think with a clear mind again.

"That painting wasn't so interesting to watch after all. Wasn't it?" Zik silly smiling said.

"Let's get better continue our "hunt" and move on Zik. I want to find the ones behind everything and taught them a lesson. A hard lesson for having me scared so shockingly!"

"Are they luckily being behind that door? What do you think Mark?" showing him the only door in the end of the hall.

"You should better be prepared little punkers for we will show no mercy!" he said aloud giving the door a strong kick. The door opened violently and something unexpected was waiting for them on the other side.

"A green house!!!" Zik said amazed.

"I have to admit it. This mansion has pretty much everything. No wonder why they choose this place to set up the prank." Mark added.

Although it was build inside the house, that part it had a glass made roof. The normal one that people uses as satellites on the green houses to use the heating energy of the sun. Of course now it was night and they were under the moonlight. They did not need any lights since the weather had become better again and the moonlight wasn't jamming any longer from the clouds. They could see by the moon light alone, sheer enough to walk. As it was much too cold outside, they started feeling the coldness on their skins. They had a quick look around them. Plants were everywhere, some lying on the dusty old tables in the middle of the room inside jars, some other were down on the flour inside their tubs and some of them were planted inside the ground. All the tips were covered by trees of any kind. Big and small, long and short. Some with branches and some without. Worth mentioning was the fact that, they were not able to see beyond the glass. The trees were covering all the glass walls around the room. Only the roof was visible and possible someone could see outside but, it was too high for anyone to reach it.

"If all this was not a prank and you really were the owner of that mansion, you would be rich now. If you were willing to keep it paying all these taxes of course. My opinion: Best thing to do, sell it. You would have a big profit and nothing to pay in return!"

"First let's try to solve the mystery behind the prank and we will see about the house Mark. It's the last thing that I have in my mind right now. I don't even consider it as prank anymore"

"Come on. Do not tell me that you have started to believe in all those craps that Kathrin believes in. If this is not a prank, then lucky you! You inherited a mansion!" They started walking inside the green house while talking. A big variety of flowers were in one of the tables in the middle of the room where they were heading, and lots of trees without foliage on their side. While Mark insisting that all this was a prank trying to convince Zik to do not believe in supernatural theories, the branches of the trees made a sound. A sound that only happens when something it's moving. The plants started growing fast; having as a result the entire cover of roof. Without the light coming from there, Mark and Zik were in the mercy of darkness.

"What now?" Mark said fuming.

"I have a flash light with me. I had it inside my pocket just in case something happens. I took it from my stuffs because I was not sure whether we will have light on our way searching for them or not." Zik said and took it out of his pocket.

It had started to become too cold as well. Zik was trying to find the on off button and then they heard a sound. It was the same sound as before but this time was creepier and louder and it was coming from behind them. He found the button and hastily he switched on the flash light and pointed in the direction of that weird sound.

"Who is there?" Mark asked trying to see at the spot that Zik illumined.

They got no answer and another sound rapidly heard behind them. This time the sound heard closer. Mark was trying to see and was asking if someone was there. Suddenly Mark felt something, a hand touching his shoulder. He turned at once and he saw himself. Something was looking exactly the same as him. It was like he was looking in a mirror.

"What the hell is going on? What is that?!" Mark exclaimed terrified without being able to believe on his eyes.

"I think that this is your prank Mark." Zik declared and did to hit the fake Mark with the flashlight but he disappeared like a smoke, before he does it.

Unfortunately for them, the weird events haven't finished yet. After the failed try to hit Marks copy, Zik turned his flash light inside the room again and in the van, the little girl from the ball room, was standing and staring on them. All happened so quickly and Zik's first reaction, was a scream continued by the falling of the flash light from his hands. The light was still lighting the little girl with the creepy smile. Both could not talk and they were just staring on her. Mark lost his temper and covered with fear. He run on her shouting courses and he tried to hit her. Unluckily, he passed through her but she did not disappear like his twin. She was still standing there except that this time her face became normal, scrapping the creepy smile. She started looked like a normal girl.

Ω

In the interim, Stefan was about to arrive at the centre of the village. He was walking; he was jumping to the rhythm of melody. The sky was crystal clear and nor dark clouds nor mist were anywhere. The sudden storm that once had come had now long gone and the moonlight was illuminating beautifully the village. Houses were left and right from any street. Wide, walkable sidewalks and little friendly looking, neighbour shops, were among the houses. Even though he wanted to look inside the shops, they all were pitch dark; resembling videogames, where the buildings all around are just projects and have no use other than this of décor. If you try walking or peeking inside, there is nothing. Stefan was closing in at the main square.

The main square in the centre of the village, was hosting the town hall and opposite of it, the local library. Both building were large, with some human kind statues on the entrances. The library's statues were holding books and the town hall's statue were holding swords. Stefan was excited and minute after minute; his thrill was rising even more. The village had indeed something magical. A kind of a feeling, which you can't really explain if you don't experience it yourself. While he was going to the entrance of the town hall, the eyes of one of the two sword holder statue moved and started monitoring him. Even though Stefan had his eyes on its direction, he turned his head the opposite side, smiled and continued walking. The statue from the left of the entrance of the town hall moved its head, trying to keep an eye on him. He was heading straight to the town hall without worries even though he had seen that weird action of the statue.

Abruptly, a shadow appeared behind him. He slightly turned his head back and with the edge of his eye, he saw the statue, standing behind him. It was looking at him with his stoned eyes and he felt a cold wind coming out of the lifeless statue. The aura of that thing was terrifying. Stefan didn't pay any attention and he did to continue the walking. The statue raised its hand and aimed for a direct hit to Stefan's head. The arm was weighting more than 50 kilos. Lucky him, the statue's effortless attempt, devoid of speed, gave the chance to Stefan to make an instinctive dodge. Should the strike be faster, Stefan would not be able to evade it and he could have been fatally wounded. Stefan dodged the statue's attack; by simply bending his head down. The statue stopped moving and started staring with query at the boy that was standing before it. The next second it started making a sound similar to the on that a young bird does when it's hungry and screams because it doesn't have any food! After the scream, Stefan took off his left headphone, turned to the statue and said to it.

"This is mean. First of all, you do not leave me in peace to listen to my music and secondly, you are an underhand_statue, trying to hit me in the back. Shame on you"

The statue this time raised the hand with the sword. Stefan smiled and lowered his head. It seemed like he had accepted his death. Although he was still smiling there was something different on him. The statue had raised its hand but it was not lowering it. It was standing there looking on Stefan. Stefan raised his eyes and looked at the statue with a look on his face like begging it to do it.

At that time, a loud sound of a car with a strong engine sounded and behind the statue, Tiger's sport car appeared. Stefan realized that they were leading the car directly to the statue and he jumped out of the way. The statue turned and in an instant it got crushed by the car, turning into millions of small stones! The car stopped and Tiger came out.

"What the fuck do you think you are doing here Stefan? Do you have a death wish or what?"

"Ha ha. I suppose I will live a little longer, right?" He answered smiling even as scratching his head.

"That's not something to laugh at. Aprilia and I had a memory loss and we had no idea where we were. You are lucky that the amnesia shock we had, happened to go away, few minutes before you got killed by that thing. Whatever it was." Tiger ironically said. Stefan was listening to him carefully and even smiled.

"I remember myself, driving behind Zik when a dark mist appeared and . . . I woke up here, few meters away from the statue. You are lucky I'm telling you again, that I saw what happened and came straight to save you."

"Thank you then my friend", he said as he picked up his headphones from the ground. But unhappily the mp4 player didn't seem to be working anymore. He pressed the play button. The screen didn't switch on but the music began playing.

"Wow even like this it is working! Sweet!" Stefan stated eager.

"Babe! Let's go and find the others. I am scared here. What was with the moving statue? Is this place haunted for real?"

"Give me one second Aprilia. Stefan, will you explain us what the hell is going on here?"

"I do not have much to say because I don't know much. I was just having a walk. Maybe the others in the mansion will know more. Follow me. I will lead the way. We kind of separated inside the mansion and because I accidently fell from a window, I decided to have a walk through the town."

Tiger exchanged looks with Aprilia not being sure whether to believe him or not. It sounded like a lie but having no other option; they took their chances and followed him. Having a two-seated car, it wasn't comfortable for Stefan to sit in the back, but their trip back to the mansion, was short.

Ω

Angelina and Melody were running through the dark hall without knowledge of where they were heading. Ultimately, they found a door. Angelina opened it and they ended up inside another room. For one more time, the mansion had them staggered. They could tell that it was the largest room in the mansion from what they have seen till now and it was bearing a resemblance of a princess room. Lots of toys could be seen all around. A big princess-like bed was in the middle of the room, with red curtains on both sides, hanging from four wooden columns. Next to the bed, was a commode, pink colored painted and a treasure chest placed in the top of it. All were pretty nice and beautifully arranged in the room, creating the perfect atmosphere of carefree childhood. They stood gazing the room for some seconds but needed not much time to realize to whom this bedroom belonged to. Chill pierced their spine.

"That is the room of the young girl from before, isn't it?" Melody scared solicited.

"Yes. It seems like it is."

'What shall we do now?"

"I do not know I don't see any door inside here. That means that we have to go back . . ." and they both knew that this was something that they wanted to avoid of any account. They started searching around, to find some clues about her. Anything could be great help in that moment. There was nothing special in this room. More or less, the room was giving the impression that was abandon and that moment, it started shaking. The entire room was shaking like when there is an earthquake.

"What is happening!?" Melody shouted!

Darkness enclosed all the rooms of the mansion and the earthquake was happening in the entire mansion. The young girl was standing in front of Zik and Mark until the darkness to cover them too. The flashlight wasn't illuminating anymore. Everything deepened in darkness and the earthquake was continuing.

Ω

Few second later, the earthquake stopped and the darkness dissolved. Mark, Zik, Angelina and Melody were all together in the living room. They all exchanged looks.

"What just happened? We were in the green house, far away from here. How come and we ended up here again?" Mark said confused.

"We were also far away from here. And after the earthquake we ended up here!" Angelina told Mark.

"I am shocked right now . . ." Zik added.

"You are not the only one my friend." Mark told him.

They needed some time to feel better and to process the situation. The mansion's main door opened and Stefan with the two others came inside.

"Hello!" Aprilia said joyfully.

"What happened here? You all look like you have seen a ghost." Tiger said looking at them critically.

"We need to talk!" Zik took the courage to talk first.

"Where is Kathrin?" Mark anxious asked.

"We will tell you what has just happened." Sadly Angelina replied to his question.

The door closed before Aprilia and was locked again as it had occurred before. That gave a shock to Aprilia but not at the others. They went and sat down in the end of the living room, where the fire place was. Angelina took the lead and began explaining, what she and the other two girls had experienced and how Kathrin had disappeared. Zik advised them to stop believing that they were part of a joke and asked explanations from Tiger about what had happened to him when he left them with no warning. Tiger said about the amnesia he and Aprilia had and that he was in no position to recall anything. Having the talking done, they reached to the conclusion, that this was not a prank and something unnatural was happening.

"Wonderful! And now what are we supposed to do? It's already midnight. Shall we go back?" Aprilia probed.

"Yes. I suppose that this is the wisest thing to do but first we have to find Kathrin. We will find her Mark!" Zik told him, trying to boost his moral.

"YES!!! WE WILL FIND MY GIRLFRIEND AND I WILL BULLDOSE THIS FUCKING MANSION!!! Mark stood up and shouted in the center of the circle that they had made. All of a sudden Mark felt unconscious on the floor. The rest eagerly reached him, trying to wake him up, but he was utterly out cold. They took him and laid him to one of the four big red sofas.

"I do not know what happened but we should better hurry and leave this mansion the soonest." Angelina suggested.

"I will stay here to protect him in case something else happens." Zik rapidly said.

"Ok my heart. We will be back as soon as we find Kathrin!" and she gave him a kiss on the lips.

They were ready to go upstairs and search for Kathrin but no sooner than they had left, they realized that something was wrong. When they first came into the mansion, there were stairs leading to the up floor and two doors, one on the left and one on the right. The one on the right was the kitchen and the other on the left was the corridor with the portraits. To their surprise, the living room was the same but bigger; more furniture and the color in the curtains was dark red instead of simple red. As for the two doors and the stairs, nowhere in sight. It was so different from before and they had just noticed it. They were searching around for a sign to lead them to the entrance but the living room was like a labyrinth now.

"What is wrong with this mansion? It seems like it doesn't want us to go!!!" Aprilia stated.

"I cannot find where we came from. With few words I cannot find where we left Zik with Mark! This is not good, I don't like labyrinths!" Angelina has started losing her mind. That labyrinth was her worse nightmare and she could not fight against it.

They continue searching around to find either them or the exit. Nothing was changing and they had no idea where they were. The only thing that broke their seeking was the sound of an old clock on the wall. They could not have possible not notice it since the sound was laughs of an insane person. The clock ranked twelve times and started laughing.

"Is it twelve o clock? Oh my God!" Aprilia said terrified.

"This is usually the time in folklores when something bad usually happens!" Angelina held.

"I don't believe in that nonsense. I want to find an exit out of here as soon as possible! Whatever it comes I will punch it so hard that it will die. PERIOD!" Tiger clearly annoyed announced. His words, made them all feel more secure. They knew that they could rely on him.

He went to the wall and took down the clock that was still laughing like crazy after the twelve ranks. Behind the clock he noticed something odd. A huge vain was on the wall. He looked at it with anger and instantly he was seeing red . . .

"What is this horse shit?" Bam! He punched it.

The wall started bleeding in the spot that Tiger had stroked it. Started bleeding and shaking. Eventually it broke and a passage was revealed. Tiger called the rest of them to follow him in there. They passed from the hole in the wall and they saw the staircase which was leading to the up floor. Tiger started rising the stairs step by step. Aprilia with Angelina were following behind him and Stefan was having a nice time listening to his music as always, following last with Melody while holding hands. They have been to the top and once more, to their surprise, a door that wasn't supposed to be there was blocking their way. Tiger tried to open it but when he touched the knob, everything became gray and he felt on the floor.

Images from the time which was locked in his memories began showing into his mind as flashback. He was watching himself driving his car following Zik. That time, he started smiling. But his smile wasn't his. It was like another person smiling using his face. Then it was when he overtook Zik and drove inside the mist. Aprilia, she was looking like a doll, without moving or doing any action except breathing.

The flashback continued. Inside the mist, he was driving all the way until he reached a cemetery. It was the cemetery of the village. It had lots of graves but no church or something alike. Tiger saw himself going to one grave over and beginning dancing a weird dance while laughing like insane. The sound of the laugh he was making was the same laugh as the clock on the wall. After having finished with the dance he went back to the car. Aprilia this entire time hadn't moved at all. She was just sitting there like hypnotized, waiting for him to come back. The bizarre Tiger switched on the engine and headed back to the village. They went near the center and after that the vision was over. Tiger opened his eyes and rapidly stood up. Everyone started asking what had happened to him and if he was feeling any better.

"I had a vision about what have happened when I left you"

"What? Are you serious Tiger? Aprilia asked him.

"I think that we were possessed by something."

"WHAT?" She said out loud.

"There is that little girl that we told you about earlier, in the living room. Maybe she has some relationship with all this." Angelina said.

"I am scared Stefan . . ." Melody said and hugged Stefan harder.

"Hey! Now that I think of it, Stefan was possessed too!" Aprilia said and looked at Stefan.

"What?" Melody startled said.

"When we found him, he was ready to be killed by a moving statue and he was smiling. That wasn't normal."

Melody looked at Stefan and burst into tears. Stefan stopped his mp4 and put it in his pocket. He hugged her and he told her reassuringly.

"I am sorry my life." And he kissed her in the forehead.

The rest of them had not understood what had happened but before they started asking, the door magically was unlocked. They all looked to see what was in the other side of the door. The sound of a girl's laughing resonated in the darkness.

"That is the little girl you were talking about Angelina?" Tiger asked her.

"I think that this is her laugh . . . yes."

He did not think of it a second time and he preceded inside the room. The others quickly followed him in fear of losing each other, like before. Tiger started cursing and challenging the little girl to reveal herself. That time the lights switched on and they saw that they were inside the little girls' room. A sound came out from the closet. Everyone seemed worried except Stefan that he had an indifferent face.

Tiger was now seriously mad. He could not accept that something had taken over his body and he seemed that he was seeking revenge. He went to the closet and opened it!

The young girl jumped over him laughing!!!

Tiger got scared and felt on the floor. The others got scared too and Aprilia also screamed! Tiger was trying to get rid of her but it was like he was touching air. The face of the young girl was scary as if you were looking a crazy person with evil intentions. She had her typical creeping smile and she was laughing like a demon. Her moves were way too fast. She was moving on him like she was on a fast forward. Then she stopped and gave him a look in the eyes! A look that could reach a person's soul.

Ω

In the meantime, Zik was trying to wake Mark up. Mark was still unconscious so making a progress was out of the question. He stood from the sofa and started walking up and down the living room. He was exhaling all the time and constantly was taking quick looks expecting for someone to show his face. All of a sudden, he realized that he should have read the diaries. If something could help them with the mansion, were those books. He went to the entrance hall and he saw the stairs that were next to the kitchen. He fast went up to his room; he took his travelling bag, emptied it and started collecting all the diaries from every room. He had every book expect of the one that, he remembered, Melody brought along in the kitchen. He left the rooms and went down to the kitchen, retrieving the last diary. He had put them all in his bag pack and he went back, where Mark was. Mark instead of being laid in the sofa where he had left him, was standing before the fireplace looking at the fire.

"Mark have you" Zik did to say but he stopped. He realized that something was not right. Mark standing there looking at the reverberating fireplace. Zik began feeling thrilled and took one step back. Mark turned slightly his head. Zik was able to see the right side of his face and he knew that this wasn't Mark. It looked like an old man more than a hundred years old. He had so many wrinkles on his face and his eyes had a grey color. His nose also had a weird shape for a human being.

"Ha ha ha ha ha!!!" The Mark thing started laughing without stopping. The non-stop sound of his laugh was becoming scarier. Zik was thinking what it would be wiser to do but out of the blue, he stopped laughing. Zik didn't want to know the reason he had stopped laughing. He started running towards the up floor where the others should have been. He was running fast without taking spare looks behind him. First time in his whole life he was that scared. The fear that thing cause him was enough to make him sweat. He couldn't run properly, his legs were shaking but he knew that he had to run as fast as he could, to be away from that thing. He reached the immense crystal door opened it and came in directly and closing it behind him.

He remained there for a second, laying his back against it. He needed to breathe because he was feeling dizzy after all this running and fear. The room was completely dark. Fortunately, even thought he had unpacked everything from inside his travelling bag, he didn't have removed the items on the side pockets. So he searched for his pocket size flash light. He panicked when he didn't find it inside and even though he wanted to curse loudly he suppressed his desire. He was now pacing up and down biting his nails. A few moments later he took a deep breath allowing his reasonable self to take a hold of the situation. Then he remembered that he placed the flash light in his pocket. He reached inside his pocket took it out and switched it on. He started walking to the other side of the room, until he saw two doors. He looked again behind him to check if that thing was following him and he tried to open the door in the right. It was the same door that it had taken Kathrin away, something that of course he couldn't know. However, the door it was locked. He heard the crystal door behind him opening and without having a second thought, he run to the other door. That one was unlocked and rapidly he went in. It was another long corridor. Zik using his flash light headed to the end of the corridor were another door was. He tried to open it. It was locked.

He didn't know where else to go and he was scared in the thought of knowing that the thing would have been there any minute. He began punching the door and kicking it as hard as he could. Suddenly the door opened from the inside and Zik looked really surprised. Angelina had opened the door for him.

"Darling? What are you doing here? Where is Mark? Why you looked so petrified?" she said and she hugged him immediately.

Zik accepted the hug and he felt safe for a second. But when he opened his eyes he saw the young girl sitting in a large princess-like bed. He took off his hands from Angelina and asked terrified for an explanation.

"There is no need Zik, my nephew, to be so scared. I know that what happened today here is out of the ordinary but I'll explain you everything as I did to your friends." The little girl said to him.

"How did you just call me?"

"Sit down Zik. You need to hear this. "Angelina exclaimed touching his shoulder.

"You are well awarded that this mansion . . . Better, this entire village is haunted and I am a ghost, obviously. It wasn't like this for ever you know. Many years ago, there was a man. A man answering to the name Lewis Anderson. He had lost everything on a terrible fire. He had also lost his right eye and half of his face was burned. He didn't have any wife or children and his parents . . . They both have died in the fire and all of his belongings had been turned into dust. Without having anything, he committed suicide by jumping over a cliff, into the sea. That's how everything started. While he was between life and death in the deepest depths of the sea, he had a vision. A spirit approached him and offered him a deal. He could have everything that he had ever dreamed and of course saving his life at the moment, with only one condition. He had to sell his soul to the spirit. In the state he was, had nothing else to lose and so he accepted the deal. He did not like the world that he was living in. So he asked from the spirit if it was possible to create him a village that only those where he would like to, would be able to live in. The spirit then, created this VILLAGE. He gave it the name Haurr. After that, he asked from the spirit to have as residents only people with good hearts and some of his friends. The spirit did what he asked for. At the end, he asked from the spirit to be pretty again and to give him power and wealth. And the spirit did that too. The first years, everything was going really smoothly. Lewis also accomplished to get married with his dreamed girl and he was living like an emperor to this mansion with his wife. They also had a child. A daughter, whose name was Felicia. Felicia Anderson. That would be me by the way. My father unfortunately could not possible know, that making a deal with a spirit like this one and selling it his soul, would have been the biggest mistake of his life. The spirit was not an innocent spirit like the fairy god mother in Cinderella . . . It had clearly evil intentions. When Lewis asked him to transfer all these good people there, he took also their souls under his command without letting them or him know. Anyone who was living in the village and had been transferred by the spirit was soulless!"

"How is that possible, to lose your soul like that?" Aprilia questioned.

"Since everyone was under his powers, he could do whatever he liked. Of course no one in the village knew about the spirit since they were thinking that they had just got lucky and have been invited by a rich person. The spirit wanted the souls to collect energy, ending in this way to rule humans. Lewis somehow learnt about his dark plans and tried to cancel the deal. Then it was when the spirit changed his way and made everyone in the village its slaves. Lewis, in order to protect his family and the people in the village, sacrificed his life sealing the spirit in this village forever. Unluckily everyone died once Lewis died but at least the spirits evil intentions had been ended. The village remained secret after this, until the day that found you. The only offspring of the family is you Zik."

"But how am I an offspring since you said that everyone in the village died?"

"When my father found out about what the spirit has done to the people of the village, he asked from my mother to leave, taking me with her. My mother left and went to the nearest village. One night, I run away to see my father. That night happened to be the same night that my father died. So I got trapped in here. You are a relative of my mother; there is no need to ask for more information. I do not know everything by the way. I just felt since the first time I saw you that you had the same blood as mine and that's why you were able to found the village."

"What is happening now? The spirit has been awakened again?" Aprilia asked.

"Somehow it did it. Yes. I can stop it but first I have to let you all out of here." Felicia rushing said.

"What about our friends?" Zik looked at her and asked.

"Your friends' are no longer alive. I am sorry. The only thing I can do, it's to help you escape from here."

"What are we going to say to their families? OH MY GOD. I have nothing to do with all these." Aprilia added troubled.

"We will see what we will do. But for now the best thing to do is to follow her." Tiger took Aprilia from the hand and all together followed Felicia.

She started opening all the doors. They passed through the long corridor and they ended in the dance room with the crystal door. They continued from there and they went to the other long corridor that had the bedrooms. Angelina asked Felicia, why the house was different before and she answered her that, this was because the spirit had the power to create illusions in their minds for a short period of time. Nothing was real and they should not worry anymore about that or anything else. She guided them until the front door and when she opened it, made a last notice.

"You have to promise me that you will never come back whatever happens. Even if I do not succeed on vanishing it, you should go live your lives!"

"Ok." Everyone agreed with her.

They went back to their vehicles leaving their entire luggage in the rooms. They had no time to stop and pick them up. They were driving until they made it out of the village. Stefan was driving Marks' car with Melody sitting next to him.

"All this which had happened today is far beyond our imagination." Zik said to Angelina while driving.

"I agree honey." She answered and her heart was dancing fast.

Ω

The sun was coming out and they couldn't understand how that was possible, since only an hour ago, the clock had sounded midnight. They thought that they had lost the sense of time. At any rate, they were almost to the village where they had made the stop about asking directions to Haurr. Tiger parked his car to the restaurant's parking area and made signal to the others to stop there too. He said that he needed some caffeine in his system. They all agreed on going inside to have a break from all these.

"I can't believe it, Mark and Kathrin died . . ." Angelina began saying mortifying when they sat in a table.

"Everything is so fucking weird. I can't really believe what happened in that village!" Tiger added perplexed.

"I will have a walk if you don't mind. I need some fresh air to clean my thoughts." Zik stood up from the table and went outside.

He was walking down the street. That village was an ordinary village and the people were already on their way to begin their day. Cars were passing next to him in the street and a man with a big mustache was opening his butcher shop. The sun was slowly coming out and as a summer day, it was also another sunny one, like yesterday. The morning air made Zik feel better. He was looking around the town and he was trying to digest what have happened in Haurr. Was it real? Or he was going nuts. For a second he had the thought that all those events never actually took place and he was dreaming. But no, inside him he knew that they had just survived from something indescribable. In his left hand, he saw a nursing home. The only one that a small village like this could have. He had a quick look around the building just out of curiosity and he was about to continue his walk. That will have happened if an old woman that time wasn't coming out with the nurse behind her calling her name.

"Felicia! Felicia! Come back here! You know that you can't go out like that. You need someone to watch over you. Come back inside please." The nurse was calling the old woman.

Zik was a bit surprised that she had the same name as the young ghost girl and he could not help but staying there and watching. The nurse saw him observing them surprised and she wondered why.

"Is there a problem sir?" She tested him.

"Erm . . . No, not really. I just heard the name of the old lady here and it reminded me a girl that I know."

"I am sure that there are lots of females living on this planet, called Felicia but this one is the only and lovely one, our Felicia Anderson. That she has an escaping issue." Said jovially to him and took the old lady from the shoulders to guide her back inside the nursing home.

Zik keep on looking at them going in, speechless.

"Excuse me! Nurse! Is that woman's' name Felicia Anderson?" while saying that a drop of sweat flowed on his forehead.

"That's my name decade's now young boy. Why my name makes a surprise to you? The old woman probed. "Did you used to live in Haurr? Zik rapidly asked.

The old woman stopped, gazing Zik. The young nurse was also surprised hearing the name.

"How do you know that name young boy?" Felicia asked him very concerned.

"My name is Zik Chorderson. I think that we are relatives but this is not the surprising thing here. I have been to Haurr and in fact, I just left from there. But before we leave, I and my friends met a young girl. A young girl with the name, Felicia Anderson!"

The old woman could not believe in her ears. The nurse was surprised for a moment and then started laughing.

"Have the two of you made a conspiracy behind my back? You should know mister Zik, that you should avoid participating to pranks like those ones with people who have serious mental health problems." The nurse said and she seemed kind of furious. She took Felicia from the hand more violently and guided her inside.

"Wait?" Zik wanted to know more since they did not gave him enough answers. Unfortunately the nurse had locked the entrance door behind her. He tried to open it but he could not do it, so he started punching it strongly with his bare fists. The sound of the unlocking sounded and two men in white uniforms opened the door.

"Is there a problem sir?" One of them asked him.

"Hi. I am sorry but I am a relative of Felicia Anderson and the nurse who was with her did not let me see her. Can we do something about it?" Zik told them seriously.

"The nurse told us that you were spoiling the medical health of Miss Felicia. She also mentioned us not let you see her. We are sorry sir. But you have to leave." And they closed the door on him.

Zik did not want to cause any more troubles so he decided to go back and ask for a backup. He went running back to the restaurant, were the others had almost finished their "breakfast". Zik run to the table and when they asked him why he was running, he told them everything he witnessed. Tiger was the first one that stood up from the table and offered to go there for some answers crackling the joints of his fists. The others did not agree at the least. But now more than ever, they had a wish of learning more about Haurr instead of going back and especially when two of their friends were missing.

All together, they were heading now to the nursing home. When they got there, Tiger wanted to go in and beat the shit out of everyone until he had his answers but Zik told him that he had a plan. Since he was the only one who had been seen, he could not go in. Luckily they did not know about the rest of them. Stefan, Angelina and Aprilia had to go in while he and Tiger should be waiting outside. It was better to do not cause any fuss in the town and to take all the possible information they could with minimal risk. Everyone, even Tiger after few objections, agreed to cooperate. Whereas the two of them went and hide in a corner nearby, Angelina ranked the belt of the nursing home. One of the two men with the white robe that Zik had seen earlier opened the door.

"Good morning. How can I help you?" the man said.

"Good morning. We are here to see Miss Felicia Anderson. I am her niece and those two are my friends. Is it the right time to make a visit now?" Angelina performing a great act, asked.

"This is weird. One man came not even half an hour ago and started asking to see her too."

"I think that I know of him. Was he around the same high as you, wearing travelling clothing?" cleverly fast asked.

"Yes! That would be him."

"He is my brother. He likes to make troubles wherever he goes. I hope that he did not do anything weird here. I am sorry if he did. I suppose to not letting him alone but he is not young anymore. Maybe I shouldn't have stopped spanking him . . . I am sure you understand."

"Yes madam. If you like you could come in. Felicia would be glad to see anyone. She is not used to visitors of course. How come and you have never came to see her?"

"We did not know about her existence. We recently learnt that she was still alive and, here we are."

The man showed to believe what Angelina was telling him was true. They headed inside the building. Nothing uncommon was there. Tall white walls were in the entrance hall and a receptionist sitting behind a desk with a fake smile and hospitality. The only room that they had a quick look was the living room for those old people. It had few tables and chairs, a couple of big couches and sofas and a big TV screen.

They followed the man on the up floor, whereas the bedrooms were. He opened Felicia's door and offered to tell them a piece of advice.

"She is not a mental healthy person. If she starts talking baloney, do not give attention."

"Felicia, you have some visitors here who came to see you. Try to be nice with them!" Said and he left closing the door behind him.

The room had nothing more than a bed, a toilet, a closet and one chair with a table. Felicia was lying on the bed, looking at the wall. Angelina approached her; she took the chair from the table and sat near to her.

"Hi. Miss Felicia. My name is Angelina. You met my boyfriend before, Zik. We also know about the Haurr village!"

"The Haurr village . . . All those years inside here, no one ever believed me. They were thinking that I was crazy." She turned her head and with tears looked Angelina in the eyes.

"No one ever believed me! I had to spend almost all my life in a psychiatric clinic after those events . . ." and she started crying.

"We have nothing in common with the rest of the people. We believe you. We experienced it ourselves. But we need you to tell us what happened back then. I think that we had been deceived by the "Spirit"." Finishing her phrase with the word Spirit, Felicia stopped crying and fear overlaid her.

"What? What is wrong with that?" Aprilia asked right after she saw her reaction.

Felicia wiped her tears off her face. She gripped from the edge of the bed and she sat normally on it. Everyone was waiting patiently for her word. Stefan from the other hand has gone near the window, not a single moment had he put off his ears the headphones. Melody made him a signal to pause and listen what Felicia had to say.

"I do not know what you have been told and by whom. I shall tell you the truth and only the truth behind my tragic past. I have spent many years of my life locked inside this clinic, after the incident took place. My father, as far as I consider, had made a stupid contract with a spirit. That contract was his soul, in exchange of his dream life. My father, Lewis Anderson, created a village and put on it all his beloved ones and every good hearted people the spirit could find, willing to live in the village. One day, he learned that the spirit was not a spirit to be trusted. Somehow he learned that it wanted to take as many souls as it was possible in order to feed and become stronger. Why it wanted that, I do not know. I only know that my father learned that everyone in the village was soulless and it was him to blame. In order to save me and my mother, he told us to leave the village as fast as we could. He believed, that only the ones living inside the village had no souls and if they were leaving it, they will had them back. That's what happened. Me and my mother left and I shall guaranty you that we took them back. A fight between it my father and the spirit started. My mother, returned in order to help him and she left me in this village alone. She never came back . . . The village for some unknown reason, I presume because of the spells, it was hidden by anybody else. No one knew it and for that cause, no one ever believed me."

"It is weird. Why the little, ghost version of yours, told us another story?" Angelina started wondering.

"Not only that. Another question is why; if the spirit wanted our souls, to let us go?" Melody wondered too.

"The spirit, had most probably taken my appearance from the years of my past. Unfortunately, I told you pretty much anything that I can remember from that time. I know nothing more . . . I am sorry. But I want to help you in any way to kill it! It took my family and my life. I want to be purified!" and by saying that a flare of fighting in her eyes gave them courage and triggered them to give their all with the aim to help her.

Inside the room, the light started fainting, as the sun was fainting behind random dark clouds. Felicia showed them the way out and thanked them. She returned back and hided herself under the covers. The minute they went out and been seen by Zik and Tiger, they were glowing.

"Really a spanking and mental incapability?" Zik complained

"Sorry love, improvising has its drawbacks"

"Anyway what happened? Why are you all so happy? Did you talk to her?" Zik asked them with agony.

"We talked to her honey. We will tell you everything that we learned. From now on, this is not only our quest but Felicia's too!"

'Ω

They were now on their way to the take the vehicles, after all the necessary explanations had been done. They all agreed on going back to Haurr and do something about the evil spirit and their missing friends. The weather was turning to be very bad again. Unquestionably, a storm was coming. Zik decided to leave his motorbike there and go with Stefan, because he wouldn't ride his bike under the sudden changes of the weather. In their way back at the village, the courage from before, was fainting away. Some of them started wondering if they should return after all, to a place that not only was haunted but also a really evil spirit was waiting for fresh food. On the other hand, they were still had no clue about the spirit. Why it let them go? Why it appeared that time? How did it lose in the past? Why did it stop if it never had lost. Those questions were still on the board, which is why they wanted to quench that fire inside them. They were scared, all of them, other more other less but the feeling of discovering the complete story, was stronger.

After having driven some miles, the gates of the village appeared. The same gates as it had been an hour ago. Nothing seemed to have changed. Slowly, the first drops of water felt in the windshield of the cars. The sky was all grey again and the wind was getting stronger. Entering the village, the sensation of being day wasn't there anymore. It looked like, it was night and really late at night. They drove until the center of the village and then . . . the engines suddenly stopped. They looked each other in the eyes from inside the cars and they all knew that was the spirits doing. They got off the cars and went rushing to cover themselves from the rain under the library's roof. Stefan left behind, under the summer rain, smiling and looking at the sky. He put his hand in his pocket and pressed the "next" button. He changed the song that he was listening to another one with title "Storm" by Vanessa Mae. He seemed like he was enjoying it but he was the only one.

"Stefan! Can you please come here sweetie? I don't want you to get sicker?" Melody called him and she was more afraid that he will get sick than the fact that they were on their own will on a haunted village.

"Sicker? What do you mean?" Aprilia gave attention to Melody's words.

"Erm . . . Sick I wanted to say . . . I misspelled it." She said frightened and started crossing her fingers.

Stefan even though he was enjoying it, he smiled and went where they were. The rain was unstoppable. Instead of stopping, it was becoming stronger. They behold at the rainy weather thinking about what to do next. A sound inside the library, tensed everyone's thought.

"What was that?" Melody asked once she heard a breaking sound.

"I will not wait here to learn it. I am going inside to beat the crap out of it!" Tiger said and opened the big double door. A thrilling sound was made by the door opening and revealed the immense interior of the library.

A huge hall appeared and gave them all, a chilling feeling at the spin. The wealth alone of the library could make anyone want to have, at least a look. Tiger calmed down seeing this and Aprilia hugged him and started kissing him. They were staring the posh floor, made out of wonderful black and granite colors. Also the roof had lots of chandeliers but not the ones using power as in the mansion but with real candles. They walked deeper and the roof there was painted. That painted room; it was where the books were. With horror they realized that the roof painting was showing a ripper, taking souls, guiding them into a river.

"I was not expecting something less than that!" Tiger mumbled and started looking for the direction of the sound from earlier.

"I think that you should relax Tiger. There is no need for this stress. What are you willing to do if you find the spirit anyhow?" Zik told him that, not because he wanted to scold him but because he really didn't have any other plan on going.

Tiger raised his left eyebrow and gave a wild look on Zik. Apparently he did not understand the way Zik mend it. Now more than ever, Tiger wanted to find the one responsible behind the noise and made him pay. Full of anger, he began walking between the library's corridors looking for evidence. Stefan was following them and Melody was browsing through the books in the shelves. Something drew her attention. All the books seemed to be the same. The title on all the books was the same "Haunted Horror". She observed that the first two letters from the first word and the "ro" from the word "Horror" were written with a red odd color. Intrigued by that, she stopped and putted her finger in the red spot on the title. Trying to see what this odd liquid was, she got shocked. The liquid was dry blood. She made a step behind ready to scream, but she didn't. She comprehended that the others had brought to a halt their steps, staring inaudibly at something.

A broken piece of a glass was lying on the floor. Apparently, it had come from a painted glass on the wall in front of them. This painted glass, was covering a secret door behind that wall.

"Hm . . . This is what I was looking for." Tiger went till the door.

"Why did that happened in the first place? Why the spirit is helping us detect secret doors? There is something that I do not like here." Aprilia was walking next to Tiger. Then a shadow moved up their heads and approached Aprilia. That was the last thing she saw. The shadow, doing a fast move, gripped Aprilia from the head and lifted her on the roof, dragging her into darkness. Her screams were sounded in the entire library. The fear in her voice made their blood froze.

"What the fuck!" Tiger left from the door and looked high up at the roof. The candles in the chandeliers began to extinguish one after another.

"I will fucking kill you! Come over here you pathetic shitty spirit!" Tiger screamed while looking on the roof for a sign. A dark smoke came, flying from the roof right on him. It pushed him hard and threw him to the door which was behind him, hidden by the glass. The weight of Tigers body and the powerful push plus the fact the door was weather-beaten, made the door brake. The secret behind the room revealed. A dusty room with a tomb on the middle showed up. Tiger was trying to come back in his senses. The push had hurt him but had made him more furious than before as well. Being a man of pride, he didn't care if it was a spirit or anything else; he just wanted to beat it.

"We have to get a place to hide. I don't want to be pushed like that. This can be fatal!" Zik made signal to the others to follow him inside the hidden room with the tomb.

The dark spirit appeared once more and directed right to Zik who was making the sign to the others to go inside the room. Zik was not looking at the time and the spirit was coming closer and closer at him. A second before it gripped him, Tiger gripped it first. He had run from the inside of the room and using his full strength combined with anger, gripped the dark smoke and by holding it, lifted it on the air. The spirit made a terribly annoying sound and transformed to a dark cloud, escaping from Tigers hands.

"Those are . . . Those are the pages, the really pages from the house keepers book!" inside the tomb, Angelina had seen over the protection glass, some pages, with the same writing character as the house keeper's.

"I need a key to open it. It's locked! Or maybe I can break it."

"Break the glass! We do not have time to waste, hiding inside here! That thing can attack us anytime!" Zik told her and was looking around to avoid another attack. Angelina with a fast move broke the glass using her elbow sheltered with her dress and took the papers that were wrapped inside. They all run outside, hearing scary screams coming from the library. The rain had not stopped so they still had to figure out where to go.

"That thing took Aprilia. I have to go back inside. I cannot let her in there!" Tiger said huffily.

"No! If you go back there, most probably you will die too. I don't want to lose another friend." Zik said to Tiger and his hand was shaking.

"I . . . This is ridiculous!" Tiger collapsed. He was really sad and above all, he could not save the only person that he had sworn to protect.

"If we defeat the spirit, maybe there is a way to take back our friends. We have to stay strong!" Angelina tried to hold his shoulder.

"I think that we have to go to the town hall as well. Those pages are not complete." Stefan said by looking at the pages.

"How do you know that?" Angelina asked him.

"I just know it. It is always like this." Stefan showed them his tongue and after he smiled at her.

"I am going at the mansion. I have to find the spirit and finish it! I don't care if I have to walk under the rain or through hell itself!" Tiger left the shed and started walking to the direction of the mansion. The rain was becoming stronger and made it all the more difficult for him to see. It was like he could not go where he wanted but only where the rain wanted him to go.

"Come back Tiger! We will figure something together! Do not be irrational!" Zik pleaded him to come back, screaming at him in fear of losing another friend. Tiger realized that the level of the difficulty he had to go through until he reached the mansion, was inhuman, so he decided to return back to the library. While he was going back, another sound like the one they had heard in the library, sounded from inside the opposite building which was the town hall.

Ω

Tiger, after hearing that sound, he started running to that direction. Zik saw him and he got a feeling about what had possible had happened and begged the others to stay there. He didn't want to lose anyone else anymore. He wanted to believe that everything would be alright and that the missing people from the party will return, but deep inside him, he didn't believe that much in his own words. He was just hoping that everything will be alright. So he had to do the best for everyone.

"Tiger!!! I am coming with you! Together we can accomplish more things! We have more chances if we work together!" Yelled and run after him. He did the first five steps and a hand stopped him. A hand so strong that was able to stop him with all that fighting will flowing inside him.

"Stefan?" He was surprised by his reaction and not only.

"You did already enough my friend. I suppose that is high time me took action as well." First time in his life, Zik saw Stefan so serious, even if the serious expression in his face appeared only for a second. After saying that, Stefan smiled again and put his headphones in his pocket. His usual smiling face reappeared. He started running in the rain and he reached the town hall in a second. Zik had stayed behind with the others looking at the rain. He did not know what to do, but he had a feeling that Stefan could take care of everything.

"Stefan!" he yelled.

"What?" a voice responded from inside the terrible rain.

"Take that!" and Zik throw the pocket size flashlight which he had in his pant pocket. Stefan caught it in the air and started running again.

Tiger was waiting under the town halls shed in front of the door.

"What are YOU doing here?" Full of surprise said.

"I am here to help!" and smiled back showing his teeth.

"Great . . . I don't need anyone's help." Ironically said and turned the knob of the door, opening the door revealing the forgotten inside of the building.

The light from the lightings was enough to see. The sunlight, was like wasn't existing at all. They didn't seem to could find something as a switcher for the lights. After searching for a few minutes they decided to move, using only the lightings light and the small flashlight which Zik has given them. The town Hall had in the inside, whatever a town hall usually has. What it was uncommon, was a painting, a huge painting on the wall in the central room which was covering it all. On the painting, a lion was preparing to eat a man while the last one was looking the lion's teeth. On man's face, horror was painted. It looked like the masks of a Japanese kabuki theater. His eyes were so full with terror and his mouth was entirely open. The lion had grabbed him and was holding him to the ground. No escape was seemed possible for the man. Moreover, Stefan noticed that the mouth of the man had a keyhole.

"Hey Tiger! Look!"

"What is it?"

"The mouth has a keyhole on it," referring to lions mouth.

"And what do you want me to do about that? I want you to find me where the noise came from. Can you do that?" Seriously said and was trying to observe something, anything that could tell him where the sound which, he had heard earlier had come from. Above their heads, a sound came from the up floor.

"Let's go to check it!" Tiger said straightaway and without losing time he went to the up floor.

"Ha ha!" Stefan followed him laughing.

Tiger made a quick turn in the hall to the stairs and started taking the stairs leading up floor, running fast. The old stairs were crackling. Stefan stopped for a second to measure the danger of the situation. He obviously didn't want to fall from the stairs because they seemed old and rotten.

After having seen that Tiger succeeded on taking them all without breaking a single step, no sooner than he saw that it was safe he did the same. Of course Tiger was going too fast looking for the noise. He wanted to find again the spirit and punish it for everything it had done. Revenge was the only word in Tigers mind at the moment. Zik's speech hadn't affected him at the least after all. He was seeking revenge and only revenge.

He was giving quick glances everywhere trying to find the spirit one more time and finish what he had started. Sometimes, some people, they have a spirit, stronger than anything else. Whether they are against an army or against something unknown, they simple don't want to give up especially when an oath in their heart has been given. They will always fight until the very end protecting their beloved ones and their pride. One of these characters is Tiger, a fighter.

"I will find you spirit. I will find you and you will regret the time you lay a foot on this world." He was screaming around all over the place and he was looking for it with passion. He had opened more than ten doors and most of them were offices, decorated with usual furniture for the circumstances. Stefan was following him normally, without running and checking better inside the rooms. Tiger opened one more door and when he did that, a dark smoke appeared, making a horrible dreadful sound.

"Aaaaaaaa!!!!!!" the scream made and that it was really loud.

Tiger got unarmed and he reacted with a scream. He walked some steps behind and he touched the wall. Scaring him was making him madder. Stefan saw the face from far and run to Tiger.

"Are you ok?" he concerned asked.

"I am . . . but this will not be, after I will finish with it."

The dark cloud which had attacked to Aprilia was on the room, flowing. They couldn't help but noticing the two dark eyes in the cloud. They were standing just few steps before the door. Both were looking at it, but neither was seemed scared. It was more like they were looking at an enemy, ready to take their revenge.

"So here you are again. What are you so afraid of?" Stefan said at himself.

The darkness was still there. Standing and observing them with its big eyes. Stefan started walking towards it and Tiger copying him doing the same.

"Are you sure that you want to go in there?" Tiger asked Stefan.

"I am sure. That thing is afraid of us, let alone it is weak and can't harm us."

"How do you know that?"

"I can tell simple by looking at it" and stepped in the room. Tiger saw Stefan walking in but for an unknown reason, he didn't want to follow him. Stefan got in the room, he walked and passed through the dark cloud. Once he did, the cloud vanished.

"You see? It was nothing to be scared about." said mockingly.

"I wasn't scared happy face!" Tiger insulted told to Stefan.

"However, this was weird. Are you a human?" Tiger gave him consecutive looks of disbeliefs.

"Of course I am!" and Stefan enjoyed it by raising in the air his grooming finger.

The noise had surely come from the room they were in. An office desk, it was all broken into pieces and a key was lying on the floor.

Apart from that, nothing else to trigger their interest was in this room. Stefan took the key and he knew exactly where to use it. He turned and saw that Tiger was looking around wondering.

"Stefan. Why do you think is this happening?"

"What do you mean?" As an answer asked him back and amazed looked at him.

"Why the spirit let us go if he wanted us and why if it was looking for the key, it let it here for us to find it?"

"I don't know. But maybe by reading the diary, we will find some answers." Having the key now, they left to go back to the painting where the keyhole was.

The floor was crackling and the sound of the rain along with the lightings, were making the atmosphere more secretive. In their way back, a door opened by itself.

"What is it now?" Tiger wondered and hardened his fist.

Stefan didn't say anything but they still continued walking to the direction of the door. They went closer and Stefan took a look inside with the edge of his eye. Someone was sitting there, on a chair behind an old desk. A shadow that was difficult to describe whether it was man or woman or even worse, a thing. He stopped for a second and Tiger saw that too. He nodded on him so as to turn the flashlight in that direction. Stefan did it. The light moved slowly until it reached the face of that. When it reached it, something really menacing was looking at them. It looked like a man but it had no nose and the ears weren't normal. They were black and they had a different shape than those of a human. The eyes of that thing were dark, apart from its irises which were red. It had no hairs, or better, you would say that it had fur as hairs.

"What the fuck is that?" Tiger couldn't stay calm before this things appearance.

"I don't know but I have a bad feeling about it. Let's go quickly to take the rest of the pages." Stefan told him with a low voice and both did to move forward.

After having done one single step, they saw that the thing had already done moving in front of the desk.

"Impossible . . ." Tiger frightened whispered.

Even with the darkness, it was still possible to see its appearance because of a lighting which stroked that very moment. Whatever that thing was, for sure it wasn't a person. It was seven to eight feet tall at least, and its body, had fur everywhere. One last thing they noticed was that it had hands and legs similar to demons as they appear in the movies. Long nails were in both hands and feet and looking furious.

"Let's go NOW!" Tiger first time in his life screamed on fear!

"I couldn't agree more now" they both started running to the ladder, without giving a single glimpse behind them. Conversely they could feel that the thing was after them and not only, that but it was also reaching them and it was reaching them fast! The ladder was ahead of them. The made out of marble, making a spiral shape stairs, all of a sudden devastated before their eyes. Now they were standing there, in the end of the corridor watching the seven meters high distance between the lower floor and them. The thing was approaching them and they had nowhere else to run to.

"This is bad." Stefan with a normal and calm voice added.

"What do you suggest us to do?"

"I do not know. But I know for sure that that thing is behind us by now" and in fact, it was right behind them.

"Ok, then I guess that we have only one option." Tiger said without turning his head back until that time.

Their next move got the thing into surprise. Tiger and Stefan at the same time turned and tried to punch the thing. When they turned with their fists to punch it, there was nothing there. They stayed to look at the empty corridor and nothing more. After having exchanged a look with their eyes, Tiger said.

"Really . . . Is it afraid of us? Because that is what I have started to believe"

"Don't know. Who knows?" Stefan said having an ignorance expression.

"Whatever, we still have to find a way to go down there."

"Let's try to jump down. It's not that high and if we hang in the edge and fall carefully, we will reduce the damage from the fall."

"I agree with you. I don't want to stay here and to wait for that thing in the size of a mountain appearing again!"

Next thing, it was them descending carefully and after hanging from the edge, they jumped with awareness down to the floor without having a single scratch. And now it was about time they go fast to put the key on the keyhole of the painting. They walked between the devastated stairs and its remains and after having cross that room, they were again in the big room with the painting on the wall. Unfortunately there was a surprise for them. The painting was different than before! The lion in the painting this time had partially eaten the head of the man who previously was praying for his life and it had left only the one quarter of the head uneaten. It was not a pleasant scene to be watched but the scariest image was not the man who has been eaten but the lion which was looking on them with its bloody eyes! It had pinned its eyes on Stefan and Tiger.

"We have to put the key in the keyhole that lies on the mouth of the lion, right?" Tiger after making a morph in his face said.

"It seems like it"

"I have a bad feeling about that lion"

"Me too . . . It is grouse with all that blood on his mouth."

"Tell me now that this is your only concern?"

Stefan looked at him and smiled.

"Anyhow. Let's do it. I have no intention of staying here forever and to I'm not afraid of a painted lion." Tiger got the key from Stefan and went to the painting. The lion was still looking where Stefan was.

"Now I hope that you will stay still." And start putting the key in the keyhole. They key reached the end of the keyhole and Tiger turned it slowly to the left one time, two times and that was it. Whatever was behind the lion's mouth has been unlocked now. He left they key there while looking at the lion.

"Ok Stefan! I did it!" and turned at him showing that he had succeeded.

"Tiger! The lion!"

Tiger felt something behind him, a movement and a cold feeling. His face covered by fear and he understood instantaneously what Stefan meant! The lion was no more just a painting on some paint but it had turned into a real lion. It jumped out from the painting and gripped Tiger who was screaming being terrified. He was trying to counter it by holding his head away from him, but the lion it was naturally much stronger than he was. Stefan was turning his head left and right so as to find something useful to help Tiger. An old chair in a dark corner, it was the only object he saw from where he was capable of fighting. He ran fast to it but no sooner than he approached it he saw that something was sitting on it, giving its back on him. So far, it had sat silently in the corner and not said a word. He didn't need to see better since by the moment he saw its back he knew. He knew that it was the thing from upstairs. He turned his head back to Tiger who was still trying to block the lion from eating him. He didn't know what to do now. The thing stood up from the chair and it turned its head quickly looking on Stefan. Its eyes were meet Stefan's. It felt like it wanted to examine him. Stefan realized now, that the chair was free and he could use it. Since the thing which was standing before him was just standing there without doing nothing, Stefan didn't lose its chance and nippily gripped the chair and started running to Tigers direction. The black creature turned his body but it still was looking Stefan as it was examining him.

Tiger was struggling because he was losing his strength and the lion was coming closer and closer on eating him. The chair stroked successfully the lions head and when that happened, the lion turned into a dark smoke and disappeared. Tiger stoop up from the floor as fast as he could.

"Thanks. I appreciate it."

"There is no need for thanking me" Stefan answered him and turned his head to the black creature.

"What the hell is going on here? What is this all about? The whole situation that we run into makes me mad!"

"I don't have the answers, I'm sorry. Now we have bigger problems than the lion. Look over there." And show him the creature which was standing in the dark corner.

"What is wrong with it? Why it's not moving? Tiger whispered on Stefan's ear.

"I don't know. But it seems that for some reason it has something for me. Go inside the room and take the rest of the diary. Do you agree?"

"Ok, if it moves call me." Tiger opened the door behind the painting and another small room appeared. It was more or less the same as the one before and it had the same tomb. He punched the glass and took out the rest of the diary. Quickly, he went out of the room and he saw that the creature was still standing there.

"Let's go Stefan!" and started running to the exit but he stopped. He turned behind him and he saw that Stefan wasn't following him.

"Come on man! What are you waiting for???!!! He yelled.

Stefan was standing there speechless. After some seconds he responded and nave to Tiger. He began running to the exit as well. Tiger gave him an unfaithful glance but both run out of the town hall.

"Hey! What happened inside there? Why did it take you so long?" Zik asked them concerned.

"Nothing to worry about!" Stefan smiled and scratched his head. First thing to do, Melody run and hugged him. She was feeling safe again, having him in her hug harmless.

"Hey Zik. Thanks for that. It was a big help" Stefan troughed the flash light at him and he caught it with both hands.

"No need to thank me man! I have bought it in case of emergency. I know it's just small one, but I'm glad that I finally got the chance to use it." he seemed glad and proud that he had taken the flash light with him, given that it seemed useful at his friends and he put it back at his pant pocket.

Ω

It was still raining outside and the weather wasn't getting any better. The wind was blowing harder than before and the nature was like a crazy caravan of elements. Water, fire and thunders, were surrounding the five young ones. Tiger told them what happened inside the town hall and gave them the rest of the missing pages. Angelina took the pages and actually, it was making sense now. She started reading it out loud while standing under the town halls roof.

"I know that what I'm doing is not safe. I shouldn't write any of this but this is one more reason why I am doing it. I had to change my diary with blank pages and to write the truth in these ones. Once again, my name is Adam Black and since I have cancer, I'm the only who leaves the spirit uninterested. I don't know why all that happened. I can only wonder that is a sort of a spell made out by some supernatural deal. The family which hired me seems to have plenty of secrets. By the day I arrived here, weird things are happening. In the beginning I couldn't explain any of this. Objectives were flying and changing locations, things constantly missing. I have realized that we weren't alone. Seeing the Family having a secret way of communication the first days, I heard about the spirit. A spirit apparently was living in the Haurr mansion. I didn't manage to get more information's but I knew that I had to be careful. During the first year, I learned, I had a cancer and I was about to die regardless my will to live. I don't know if I did well. But I didn't go to the local doctor but in a doctor in the nearest city. For some reason, I couldn't trust anyone in this town. But the money was good and I had no reason to leave my job and the town, only by having suspicions. I needed compelling proves if I wanted to leave Haurr. After some years, a little girl was born in the family. The little Felicia it was a blessed child. You could say that she was overflowing by warmness. After her birth, the problems, the real problems, began and this is where I learned the truth. I saw one day the spirit of the house. Nobody had ever seen it. But I knew. I knew that it was even getting stronger only by hiding. It was taller than the tallest man in the village and it had a black fur. Only its appearance was enough to make me feel the terror of what was coming. I talked with my boss Lewis and I told him everything. He told me that I shouldn't have put my nose in the family's affairs but he also thanked me that I at least went to him first. After that, during the following year I didn't see any action to been taken by Lewis against the spirit. Nothing at all, like I never told him. I knew that something was odd since the very beginning but now my suspicious were growing deeper. Not knowing whom should I trust anymore, I took the decision to start my own research. Did I have any reason to do that? I don't know, maybe it was the excitement of doing something different just for a change, or maybe I just wanted to act heroically and save someone before I die. I don't really know, but what I know is that I wanted to do it no matter what. So I did. I started an investigation, even if the family wasn't talking about it; I started discovering things on my own. One day, in the library, I found what I was looking for. It was a book different than any other book in the library. A book with the title Haunted Horror. Its title was written with blood and the pages inside were covered by dust. I took it and I started reading it. What I discovered it was a shock. It was written in the book that, this spirit was a very dangerous spirit that wanted to come back to life. It had to make a soul trading deal with someone desperate. After that, the more souls it would absorb given by the person with whom it made the contract with, the more the chances to return. Something as evil as that, couldn't live twice I though. For some unknown reason, the spirit had to keep the contract from the deal and that's how I found it, folded, inside the book.

I knew now what was going on. I didn't want to believe that my good friend Lewis could have done something like that. Shall I tell him that I know or not? What if he wanted the deal and come after me in order to silent me. But if he doesn't know about it, shouldn't it be better to know it? It was a tough decision to take but in the end I decided to take my chances. After talking with Lewis, the surprise in his eyes was revealing everything. He didn't know about the dark plans of the spirit. Now we were two and together we had better chance of stopping it. I will continue the writing after taking it down. Just in case that something happens to me, I will have the remains of what I learned. Now I'll hide what I've learnt so far in two places, so as the spirit cannot find them. One it is going to be in the library and one in the town hall but both will be safely hidden. As a last thing, I reached a conclusion, watching the spirits' actions. I think that it controls fear. Somehow it can turn your fears into reality and if the fear becomes stronger than you, then you may lose your life. If I am right, being fearless will help me to kill it easier!"

"That is all." And Angelina wrapped the pages and put them in her pocket.

"Ok . . . We learned about the history of what have happened here, but we still have no clue of how to stop it." Zik said cattily.

"What about the personal books that you are carrying on your back bag?" Melody asked Zik.

"I have totally forgotten that I had them with me all this time." Zik unzipped his back bag and along with the others, began reading in fast forward the pages. Unluckily they were all dissatisfied. Those were only diaries and nothing more. There was not even a single reference to the Spirit.

"That's too bad . . . Now that I think of it, if the fear part in Adam's pages is true, then we have a chance to do not lose anyone else from now on, I believe." Angelina conceded.

"Erm . . . Can I say something?" Melody shyly asked.

"Of course Melody, what is it?" Angelina urged her to talk.

"If the spirit had collected so many souls, why it didn't make it to its reborn?" and she hold Stefan's arm stronger.

"She is having a point! Most probably, they have found a way to stop it but maybe they did something wrong that is why it's not dead and it also happened whatever happened here." Angelina retorted.

"Those are lot of maybes." Tiger said. Zik was standing silent next to him and he was thinking. After a second he took the initiative to talk.

"What's your fear Tiger? What are you afraid of?"

"What do you mean? That I am scared of that thing?"

"No. I don't mean that at all. But what is that that you are really scared about?"

"Lions!!!" A tiger is afraid of lions!" Stefan said eagerly. Tiger seemed annoyed by his interference but he continued the talking with Zik.

"I had a fear for lions since I was young. I have seen that documenter on the TV about how strong and fearful animals are and since then I am afraid of them. But that's a reason why I decided to be called tiger. It's the only animal in the animal kingdom that can equally battle lions."

"I suppose Kathrin was afraid of darkness. Mark he was afraid to lose his self. That's why he was studying psychology. He had a fear that one day, he will lose himself and if that day ever had to come, he wanted to be able to fix it. I know because he expressed me one day."

"What do you mean by all that my heart? The stronger the fear it makes it easier for it to kill you?" Angelina asked him and waiting for his answer.

"I believe so. If you think about it, all the things that happened are relative. And about the house that it was different as you told me. Someone has to have this fear."

"I did. I was really scared of the house never letting us go and I was thinking a scenario on my head. When I saw Kathrin disappearing, I remembered one movie I had watched where an earthquake came to pass and then nothing was the same." Angelina poorly added.

"That doesn't explain why everyone else is seeing someone else's fear? Why for example we all experienced that dark hole ending up at the same place but when Zik came to find us hunted by Mark-thing, he was seeing the normal house and us had to go through a labyrinth?" Tiger popped up another hard question.

"It has the power to make your fears into reality. That mean that the scarier you get, the more powerful the effect of your fear becomes. I don't know it for sure of course, but this is what I believe. I am no scared of lions. So when I hit it disappeared. Remember?" Stefan explained to Tiger and smiling gave him a touch at his shoulder.

"So. Angelina was extremely scared and her fear, even if we weren't together, dragged us all. Of course later, when Zik when out to find us, she was already relaxed in the room and the fear had already broken. Hm . . ." Tiger have starting to understanding what was happening, as did the others too.

"I got sick and tired with this story. I am going to find my girlfriend and take her back. I don't want any objections on my decision anymore!" Tiger madly said and went into the storm.

"Where are you heading?" Zik asked him putting his hands on his mouth making his voice louder.

"I am going back to the mansion. It's obvious that everything started from there and everything will end there!" and continued walking inside the storm until he faded away.

"What shall we do Zik? We've got nothing from the diary about how killing it or how did they stopped it in the first place." Angelina said and her eyes revealed the agony she was feeling.

"I do not know my heart. Do you want to go along Tiger's way? He isn't going to wait for us and you know it. I personally don't want to lose another friend."

"I suggest that we go back at the mansion and decide what to do afterwards. What the two of you believe? Angelina asked Stefan and Melody.

"Stefan?" Melody looked at Stefan. He smiled and nodded.

"The storm is strong for sure but we can pass through it. Everyone lets hold hands as to avoid separating from each other!"

Zik took Angelina's hand. She with her turn took Melodies hand and Melody gripped Stefan's hand. They began walking inside the storm, trying to find out the right way of going to the mansion. The wind was too powerful and pushing them away. They could barely walk and the rain wasn't making it any better. Thunders were consecutively striking and winds were pushing them back. The houses now couldn't anymore been seen. The storm was blocking any vision of the buildings. It was like they have felt into a sandstorm in the desert where you can see nothing but sand. In their situation, they could see nothing but rain. It literally whipped them. They were just walking slowly into the unknown.

Ὠ

Tiger had succeeded on reaching the mansion. Being alone he was moving faster than the others, and he had a purpose. He wanted at any cost, to find his girlfriend and take her back. Whether he will find her or not, one thing it was certain in Tiger's mind. The spirit shouldn't live anymore. He was wrathful, seeking for justice. Without feeling the slightest fear he was ready to end this. He knew that being fearless now, he had the upper hand.

He arrived at the entrance and he passed between the opened rails. The moon was supporting him with a little light but he didn't need more. The biggest problem for him it was the storm which made it all the more difficult to see every minute. His clothes were totally wet and he was feeling cold. However, he didn't have any intention of giving up. He wanted to save his girlfriend and give "a lesson" to that spirit. He was stepping inside the dirty mud of the ground around the mansion. It felt the ground subsides under his feet but he gathered all his powers and continued without falling. Being stubborn, made him champion of the English boxing champions in his league. This was nothing for him compared the training he had to go through before the championship. Although being tired, he made it at the door. The shed was providing him protection from the rain now. He shook his head a couple of times to clean his head from the rain. He didn't have lots of hairs having the short haircut of a boxer and it wasn't time consuming to get them dry.

He was standing in front of the door now. He was feeling week and tired, but inside him a fire was burning. A fire warm enough to made him want to end it now. He touched the knob and tried to open the door. It was locked. He left the knob from his arm and screamed.

"Are you scared now? Let me in Spirit!" an all-out angry voice came out from his mouth. The door then opened with a strong wind blasting as a background. Before his eyes there was the living room as they had left it. He stepped inside looking around for anything unusual. He did some steps in the mansion and he stopped. She was standing there. Before his eyes, the young girl named Felicia Anderson. She had the creepy smile on her face and she weren't moving at all. Tiger felt Goosebumps on his body but he got over it right away. He stopped and his eyes lingered on her madly. Her eyes were bleeding and now more than ever, she looked horrific. She had turned her head slightly on the right side and she had her eyes wide opened. Tiger watched her for a second froze and then he incredulously said.

"You took that form again, hu? Give me my girlfriend back NOW!" he raised his voice tone.

The girl was still standing there without reacting in the least on Tigers intimidations.

"I see . . . You want to do in on the hard way. So be it!" Tiger shook his fist and step by step was crouching closer and closer to her. She was still there, doing nothing at all. Tiger felt himself frightened for a second but he supressed the feeling because he knew that if he wanted to win he just had to do what he always used to do.

"The only thing I need is one straight punch and nothing more. One straight punch on her face and I will knock her down unconscious if not dead!" he was thinking in order to keep the fear out of his mind. He was standing one step before his fist could reach her. He stared at her bloody eyes and took the stance of his boxing style. Made a step in front and said out loud.

"That's it! Farewell!" he punched her with all his strength, exactly at the center of her head. His muscles vibrated because of the strength he used. It was a successful hit. The girl was still standing there, looking at him having his punch on her face. She didn't bleed not even a little and she didn't even move. Tiger felt that time fear taking over him. Striking this punch should have normally knocked her down for good. But no, she was standing there like nothing happened, no reacting at all, in the insanely powerful punch which she had just taken.

"This is ridiculous!" he said and his voice was trembling. The little girl started disappearing. Her body was like being taken by the wind and its place was taking a dark shadow taller than Tiger. In the end, the thing from the library was standing in front of him instead of the little girl and the punch was in the high of that things' navel. With its two dark bloody eyes looked at him and in an instant it caught his right hand which was on it. Tiger was remaining speechless cause of the panic and fear he was feeling now. He was completely helpless. He couldn't talk or move. The thing raised him from the ground and was holding him in the air from his hand. Tiger didn't know what to really do that time. Suddenly it felt an inhuman pressing power at his right arm and he witnessed in fractions of a second, before his very eyes, the extirpation of it. The spirit had uprooted it and thrown it at the floor. He felt as well.

"AAAAAAAAAAAAAAAA" he started screaming using all his strength! He was crying and he was watching his blood spreading all over. He tried to hold his hand but the view of his ripped apart hand it was making him hurt more. He was constantly losing blood. He was ready to faint but he knew that if he did it that would mean the end of his life. The spirit in its true form was fearsome and indescribable strong; Tiger gathered the remains of his strength and stood on his feet with great difficulty. He wasn't standing normally since he had lost almost all his powers but he still had some will inside him. He turned his back and woonded he began running until the door. Not looking behind, not stopping at anything. At this point, he wanted to escape. He managed to reach the open door but he fainted once he stepped at the threshold.

Ω

On no account, the weather was becoming better. Summer weather isn't always good, but this time, that particular conditions of clime, it was like no summer at all. Somehow, Zik, Angelina, Stefan and Melody managed to make it till the mansion. They were wet until their bones and physically too tired. The way until the mansion, without the storm it was supposed to be not more than ten minutes, but they needed at least twenty five, walking under those circumstances. The storm in the mansion it was a little bit calmer. They passed between the gates rails and they quickly run at the mansion to protect their self's from the rain. The door was opened but the lights weren't on. Zik first went and tried to switch them on but to his surprise he couldn't find any switch.

"Stefan. Can you help me find it?" Zik heavily breathing after this try to come there, asked.

"Sure" and he followed him inside. Zik switched the flash light on after taking it out of his pant pocket and started illuminating the walls for a switch. He realized that there was none switch. The chandeliers apparently were working only by the spirit.

"Shit!!!" he yelled and he gave a punch at the wall. The lights then switched on.

"Finally!" Zik said and he felt that he would collapse. Everyone was extremely tired and no one could tell how many hours had passed since their last sleep.

"I . . . I need to warm up. I feel too cold . . ." Melody began shaking and she was paler than usual.

"You must get sick because of the rain and the fact that you had no rest the last twenty four hours didn't help. Let's find you something quickly." Angelina took her and they started walking inside, leading to where the fireside was. Stefan lifted her in his arms. Angelina was also trying to provide her warmness.

"We should not forget that there is a big chance the spirit to be around here. Have your eyes wide open for it!" Zik warn them while was trying to stay on his feet. His body as everyone else's, it was too weak and barely making it to stand.

"By chance, we will take our things back too. Maybe I can find something that we can use to kill it on my traveling bag." He though and followed the others, covering their backs.

Angelina and Stefan laid Melody at the sofa which was near the fireplace and they were trying to find matches or a lighter to set up a fire. There were woods in it but nothing around them would help to have this fire on.

"I am sorry . . . I am such a trouble!" Melody started crying.

"Don't say that my heart. It's not your fault and you will see. In the end everything is going to be alright. Just relax and we will try to find something to warm you." Stefan was holding her hand with his right hand and with the left was touching her hand consoling her.

"Stay here. I am going to bring our luggage's here. I am sure that we have a lighter somewhere there and on top of it she can change clothes. Wearing the wet ones isn't good by any means!"

"Wait. Splitting up now is not a good idea honey after all; it would be wiser to stay together." Angelina stopped him by saying that. Zik didn't know what to do. He wanted to go upstairs and bring everyone's traveling bag there. But he was afraid as well. Angelina saw the hesitation in his eyes and she felt that he wanted to help him on bringing an end on this story.

"Ok. I changed my mind. I believe that you are capable of going upstairs without something bad happening to you but I am coming too. You will need help and above all you seem like collapsing. I don't want you to die at any cost!" Angelina solidly said. Zik seemed to don't like the idea of Angelina going with him at first but having a second though, he agreed.

"Ok, I feel more secure should you be with me. I believe that I can protect you anytime if I have you by my side my angel and it is true that I don't feel really well. I may end up needing your help!" Zik gave her a kiss at her lips to show her his love.

"Are the two of you going to be ok?" Angelina asked Stefan.

"We will survive. Just bring us something to warm her up." Stefan had not lost yet his habit of smiling. He seemed strong even after all these troubles they have been through. Angelina and Zik felt the will to survive for first time coming from Stefan. Usually he was just following without really participating in the company's affairs and his spirit even if he was smiling had always something, hollow. Now, something was different on him. Something was making him livelier.

They left the living room and they headed at the first floor. They had their eyes wide open for the spirit. They were pushing away all the bad thoughts and fears, thinking only about taking their things back at first and then they had in mind to find a solution to resolve this. They started climbing the steps. Each one of their steps, was making enough sound to make them stop and detect around, for odd actions, only for few seconds before they start moving again. Finally, they made it at the up floor. Everything it was exactly as they had left them before they leave. Zik went fast at his room and took his traveling bag. He also packed some things that Angelina had taken out of it. Angelina was standing at the door. Waiting and securing.

"I am ready. Let's go take Stefan's luggage and we are leaving this floor at the soonest." Zik said to Angelina after he had packed everything in the bags and starting carrying them. Now they were ready to go at Stefan's room. That time they heard a scream. The scream appeared to come further than the crystal room.

"What was that?" Angelina said and looked at the big crystal door which was ajar. Another sound sounded then, and the chandeliers at the end of the corridor erupted. The same started to happen at every chandelier at the corridor. One after another, they were exploding and darkness was taking their place. Finally, the last one over their head erupted too.

"Aaaaa" Angelina made a scream and Zik protected her, using his body, from the falling glasses throwing her down on the floor. The glasses didn't cause any wounds at Zik but now they didn't have any light to see apart a small gleam of light which was coming from the lightings out of the window.

"Shit. Why did that happened now!?"

"Honey, are you hurt?" Angelina worried asked.

"No, I am ok sweetheart. I think that I have the flash light that I lend at Tiger and Stefan at the Town Hall." He put his hand on his pant pocket and took it off. Once again, he was happy for having it with him. He switched it on and now they were able to see again. He helped Angelina stood up from the floor and he pointed at Stefan's room, he shall so light the way. Being more careful and quiet this time, knowing that the lights didn't break up by it self's, they went into the room. Zik made a signal to Angelina to close the door behind her. It was safer now. They found one big luggage where the stuffs of Stefan's and Melody's were. They haven't unpacked anything so they took the suitcase and making no noise, they opened the door again quietly and they were about to exit the room.

"Aaaaa!!!" another scream sounded from the same direction as before. Angelina eyes popped out of their sockets and stretched her ears. She looked surprised!

"Zik! That's Tigers who is screaming!" and she put her hand off her mouth.

"Really? Oh my God! No!" Zik didn't want to lose another friend and he felt terrible that he could hear his friend screaming like he was hurt.

"FUCK! What shall we do now?" Zik was confused. He wanted to go and help him but he also had to go back to help Melody.

"Ok, to split up isn't a good idea right now. Let's go back at fast and then we will run into there. Do you agree my heart?" Angelina was waiting for his answer. He took one second to think. He looked at her and then he looked at the crystal door. He shook his tooth hard and said.

"Alright! But we have to come back here as fast as we can. Screaming like this it means that he is in great pain!"

"I don't want him to die either dear." Both had a glance at the crystal door while they started running to the opposite direction to deliver the luggage at the others. Their steps now, sounded in all over the mansion. They had no reason being careful any longer. They were aware that the spirit had noticed their presence. Zik had left Angelina to go front and he was following right behind her. She was at the steps now and she started descending two at a time, holding at the same time the wooden sidebar. She was at the last stair but something made her do an unforeseen halt. Zik almost got to fell on her stopping like that.

"What happened my heart? Why did you stop like that?"

"It is here." And she moved her head in the side and before her the spirit with the appearance of the little Felicia girl, was standing, only some meters away, from them.

"It obviated us after all . . ." Zik whispered at Angelina.

Ω

She was standing only few meters away from them. Wearing a white long dress and having her hairs cough in the edge of a long ponytail. The look in her eyes was . . . indescribable, as it also was her smile.

"I have to admire it. The two of you turned out to be a bigger problem than I had imagined." the young Felicia said at them with an admiration in her voice.

"What?" Angelina obviously bewildered asked.

"When I send you the e-mail the first time, I couldn't possible imagine that you would be bringing your friends here with you. Your friends ended up being spirited stronger than the two of you but now I see that you got stronger than the first time you stepped your feet in my village." She was talking like she was proud or something likewise. They were both confused hearing her speech. Angelina had the need of asking what it was this all about.

"What do you mean by saying that spirit? Yes we know what you are and what your powers and purpose are!" she said it with a loud voice and she wanted to achieve fear at spirits face but this didn't happen.

"Hahahahaha" she was laughing like a little girl but even thought it was an innocent laugh, it had a bad taste.

"What is so funny to laugh about?" Zik join in the conversation.

"I am laughing with you of course! Let me first answer you the first question. If you know already, I need souls so as to get stronger. Nobody was coming to Haurr because it was a village made by the wish of Lewis so I couldn't get anyone to live here since Lewis death. But I got really lucky when I found out that Felicia had a cousin which she went to visit her one day. After that day, I gave my all to find someone with a strong spirit and bring him or her here. That's how I got to you. Compared to everyone else in this family Zik, you were the youngest and the strongest, so I decided to take you."

"And how the hell did you know that I'll take the bite of the mansion? How did you know in the first place to send an e-mail? That's insane!" Zik interrupted it while speaking.

"I don't only see the fear silly boy; I can also see your deepest desires and made them into reality! How do you think that this village got build? I create it from Lewis wish! *You wanted to find a great house in the country side. That suited me **perfect**!*" and its voice had started changing and becoming heavier and wilder as the tone becoming louder. Angelina did a step back and she touched Zik's chest. She got scared by the changing of the tone in Felicia's voice. That happened only once, she continue the talking with a normal girls voice.

"I can sense it you know. I can sense that you start feeling scared. When you first came here, I was disappointed. The two of you, were two spirited week and you also didn't have the emotion of fear. Fortunately, you brought your friends with you. Oh, I can assure you that they were stronger than you and they were already scared! The first couple, plain sailing. They were so scared and their souls . . . Yummy, delicious! I could collect enough power only from the two of them but you made me the favor and after I had no use of you, you returned! Isn't it that stupid? You were actually thinking that you can defeat me? You didn't even know what I was!"

"Enough!!! I am sick of you! We returned In order to stop you and your plans." Zik yelled at it.

"My plans? What do you suppose my plans are **ZIK**?" and the tone on its voice changed once more.

"You want to kill and to return in this world. As I have realized until now. You are just an image in this world or something alike!" the conversation was becoming stronger.

Young Felicia looked at them for a second with saying nothing.

"However, *I just wanted to thank you for getting stronger and making your spirits more powerful. Now I can take you too and you can forget about leaving Haurr!*" those were the last words that the spirit said. It started changing and becoming taller and darker until it looked like the thing that Stefan and Tiger had met in the library. Angelina was observing the transformation and she felt Goosebumps in all over her body. Zik was speechless having the same reaction as Angelina. The young girl's image was disappearing. Dark fur was covering gradually her skin and she was becoming taller. Now a beast was standing before them. The appearance itself of that thing was frightening and impressive. After the transformation, it swigged its head twice and stopped it nailed on them. That it was a moment of stillness. Zik swallowed hard and Angelina was breathing faster. They knew that they were scared now and anything was possible to happen. The spirit made a step and got closer to them. It was about to do another one and doing some more steps it would be able to reach them but the sound of someone running made it stop. It turned to see what that noise behind its back was and he got into surprise catching sight of Stefan holding the fireplace's tong and hitting it at the side. Doing that, the spirit turned into darkness and fainted away.

"Oh god Stefan! You saved us!" Angelina run and hugged him. She held the fear of having the same fate as her friends and now she felt that she could breathe normal again.

"He he. Come on now. I didn't do anything. You are my friends and I caught it unguarded. After all I need dry clothes and something to set up the fire in the fire place. I was coming to found you when I saw it and being prepared I acted."

Zik descent and the last step and thanked Stefan by giving him two touches on his shoulder.

"Thanks man. If you hadn't showed up, I don't want to consider what would have happened."

Stefan smiled back and told them to hurry and go back because Melody was becoming worse. So they did, they went at the living room, were the fireplace was and Melody was shaking on the sofa. She was cold and she needed immediately new and dry clothes. Stefan opened his suitcase and took of a dress and some under wears. He pleaded with them to do not look for a second until he had Melody dressed. At least, having dry clothes it was far better that wearing wet ones. Nonetheless, they still needed to go and find out what had happened to Tiger.

"Stefan, we heard Tiger's screams on the up floor. I really want to go and find him. If he is still alive I want to help him. Are you going to be ok by yourself here?"

"Certainly. Are you sure that you want to go alone?"

"You have to stay here anyway to take care of Melody. I'm sure that I will be fine. The only thing that I have to do is to clear my head and to have no fear!"

"I am coming with you too! Forget about going all alone in this house." Angelina said at him and you could tell by her face that she meant what she said.

"Of course my heart. Stefan, if anything happens, you can call us. And he took out from his pocket his mobile. It searched for reception but no surprise, it could not find any.

"I should have known it. Of course and it has no reception in here." He seemed pissed off because he needed the phone but Stefan calmed him down.

"We are going to be just fine. Go and find Tiger!" and he urged him to hurry. Zik realized that he should already have gone, but first he needed a weapon. He run in the kitchen and started looking for anything useful. After having opened some drawers, he found a well sharped big knife.

"That should do." and he turned to leave. Before he does it, he felt that someone was behind him. He felt fear again and that moment a hand touched his shoulder. He made a weak scream and turned fast holding the knife ready for arsenal.

Ω

"Baby, it's me" Angelina told him before he stabbed her. Zik calmed down seeing that it was her and lower the knife.

"You ripped the soul out of me. I thought that it was the spirit. Do not come like this, I could have stabbed you my heart." he did not want to do something reckless and stab his own girlfriend. Angelina apologized for being behind him like this and she advised him to go.

They went out of the kitchen and having switched on the flashlight they headed upstairs. Once again, their steps were careful, not wanted to give away their position at the spirit in case it did not know where they were. Every step seemed like a year now. They wanted to go faster to save Tiger but they didn't want to go in an all-out battle with something that they still had no idea of to how stop. After several seconds have passed, they were at the second floor, directing this time at the crystal door. The broken glasses from the chandeliers were everywhere and they were trying not to step on them so as not making any noise. Even though they were really careful, they stepped on some of them but the crashing sound was tiny and they didn't bother. Zik was lighting periodically with exact same order firstly the floor, then ahead of them and lastly around them just in case something appear. Having walked that utterly long corridor, they arrived at the end at the ball room's door. It was still slightly opened.

"We have to proceed cautiously inside . . ." Angelina, after the last time she was there, she was thinking it twice going in.

"That is the ball room where Kathrin has been taken by the spirit right? It's natural being scared of that room. I would feel the same sweetheart but remember that fear makes it stronger, that's why you should show no fear now and go inside. You can be stronger than it my heart!"

"I know. I have to clean my thoughts first . . ." She needed a few seconds to calm down and then they went in. Without lights, that room wasn't so bright. Zik lighted the room for a second, to have a general idea how it looked like and then he turned the light at the two doors in the other side of the room. They couldn't hear anymore Tiger's screams. They went near the doors and stood there till they've reached a decision in which way should they follow.

"I can't hear him anymore. Damn, I hope that he is fine!" Zik was disappointed and mad for he wanted to help him but now he didn't know if he was still alive and that it was a though he didn't like.

"I am suggesting going this way" Angelina showed him the door on the right. It was the door where Kathrin had been taken from the spirit.

"Why do you say that?" Zik asked her pointing with the flashlight that door.

"That is the door where Kathrin disappeared. We know that if we go from the left door, we will go at the children room. But from here, we have no idea what lies behind that door. Most probably Tiger is there."

"I would like to yell and ask where he is right now but I'm afraid that the spirit will notice us if we do that."

"If it hasn't done it by now. I think that it knows everything once we are inside its magic, but anyway. Let us continue, shall we baby?"

"I trust you on this one my love! I am guessing that you are right. It may know everything or it may feel everything, since as you said we are inside its magic. We will go in there and I hope that will be safe!" Zik said and opened the door. He did it slowly and carefully as to not cause any noise. He didn't open it all; he just left a small opening, small enough where only his head was able to pass. He also passed the flashlight and he lighted the place. He had a glance around and he saw steps with a downhill direction.

"I think that is safe. There is an old staircase there, which leads deeper down." He said whispering. Angelina agreed and he opened the door more and they both passed through it. They started getting down. At the beginning, they presumed that once they were at the second floor, those stairs will lead them on the first floor but they were wrong. The stairs were longer than the other ones and they were going deeper, underground. No sooner they arrived they realized that they were in the basement. That part of the mansion, it was different than the rest of it. It had no painted walls or any chandeliers for the light. Instead of that, it had torches on the walls. It looked like an old catacomb, or like the old cellars, that the people used to use centuries ago. Moisture and frost completed that inhospitable place.

"My heart, do you want to set fire on one of the torches?" Zik whispering asked her.

"I don't think that we have something to set the fire on. Or do we?"

Zik searched his pockets. He had nothing apart from the flashlight, his motorbike and house keys. Angelina searched in her pocket too but with in vain; she couldn't find something they could use.

"I just do not know how much energy the flashlight still has. I don't want to run out of energy in case I will need the most." Zik explained in this way, why he wanted to set up fire on a torch.

"However, we can still use the flashlight my heart. But I have a question. Don't you think that this is too far from where we heard Tiger's screams? Think of it, it couldn't be that far, right?"

"You got a point I don't . . ." he couldn't finish his phrase; from the end of the corridor they heard a noise. At the end of it, they could discern something like a cellar. The flashlight's beam, couldn't reach far enough to see what was in there. Although they didn't know why they have heard Tiger's screams closer the last time, they decided to go on. Being extremely alert, they walked cautiously as before. Exploring the spooky basement of the old mansion, was making it all the more difficult to keep their heads clear from every fear. One by another, they were passing by the torches and they were going closer and closer at the cellar. The light was helping them see better what was in there. After having come close enough, they saw what was in there. Big barrels, probably wine ones appeared at first. They could hear nothing from the cellar. Deadly silence overwhelmed the atmosphere. Zik went and touched one of the barrels. He caught the tap and twisted at an attempt to see what it had inside. This one was so empty that not even one single drop came out of it. He went to try another one, but Angelina made him signal to move on.

"What are you doing? Is it really the time to do that?" she whispered when at the same time she was scolding him.

"No, it isn't but I wasn't sure if those barrels had wine or something alike inside . . ." and she understood that by saying that he meant blood.

"Ok, I see why you wanted to check it. Even yet if it's like that, we have to keep moving my love." And she wrapped her hand around his waist pausing for a moment and standing still searching comfort to each other. Then they kept walking surrounded by barrels and a stingy smell of something decayed.

For sure where they were now, nobody had it cleaned for ages. They were examining everything they could around them. They passed under a curved, like a door, stoned wall and they were watching now a long series of bottles on shelves.

"Let us keep moving please." Angelina whispered once more at Zik pulling him tide to her. Zik continued walking and then he noticed something. He turned the flashlight into a red spot which was on the floor.

"What is that? It seems fresh" he wondered.

"I really do not want to know!" Angelina said and tried to keep him away from it, but Zik took his hand off her and went to the spot which seemed like a bloodstain. He smelled it and he drew back his head because of the smell.

"This is blood! And not only that but it is also fresh!" He said and got away from it by doing some steps behind.

"Oh my God!" Angelina said and put both of her hands in front of her mouth covering it because in a different case she would have screamed. Accidently, because of Zik's sudden reaction, the light from the flash light was showing them Tiger, who was at the end of the room, bounded by chains on the wall and missing one arm. Zik saw that the spot of blood he had spotted wasn't the only one. There were more on the floor and in fact it was all coming from Tiger! He turned the light right on him and he had been speechless watching him being in that state. He was thirty meters ahead of them and where he was, it seemed different than the room they were. They closely got near him. For a second time, they passed another stone arch, like the one before.

"What is that smell?" Angelina said covering her nose.

Zik lighted the place. On Tiger's left a room with a small window with iron cages appeared. He wanted to go and check what the disgusting smell was but first he had to help his friend. He asked Angelina to hold the flash light so he shall free him. Tiger was unconscious or at least that's what they though. Zik caught Tiger's hand and examine the chains they were holding him. They weren't made from something he could have seen never before. The material that they were made of, didn't exist or he had never seen it in his entire life. It was a black hard but at the same time liquid thing, strong enough to hold a person like Tiger on the wall evidently. No keyhole or anything to testimony how to unlock it.

"It's a waste of time." Tiger said dismally, with a soulless voice.

"My friend, you are awake. Are you hurt? What happened?" Zik asked him concerned wanting to know how he ended up like this.

"I got imprisoned by the spirit . . . It uprooted my arm . . ." the sad emotion of losing his arm made him started crying. For a boxer to lose his arm, meant the death of his career.

"This is a minimum damage my friend. You could be dead! Come on, we will figure out a way to take you from here!"

"It is of no use to break those chains. I saw the spirit using parts of his skin to make them. I doubt if you will be able to release me. Since the time it left, I have been trying to escape but with no success. I have no more power in me . . ." Tiger was utterly defeated.

"No way! I am not accepting to lose you too. When did it leave, do you know?"

"It left some minutes before you show up. As I understood, it wanted to hold me inside that stingy room, but for an unknown reason, it left hurrying that's why I am here."

"How do you know that it left in a hurry? Did it tell you something?" Angelina asked him, everything they could learn now would be a piece of help.

"No . . . For a mysterious reason, I can sense it. I feel connected with it. Do you remember Angelina when I touched the knob of the door and I had a vision of what had happened to me and Aprilia?" Angelina nodded her head positively.

"Well, ever since then, I can feel its present and feelings. I don't know if it knows that I can feel these, but I can tell you that it is scared now. While it was carrying me down here, something changed in it, something made it to want to come and find you in a haste." Tiger finished saying and started spitting blood from his mouth coughing at the same time.

"Take a breath my friend. Do not tire yourself. Angelina, what shall we do? We have to take Tiger from here, he is about to die.

Maybe it was all wrong that we returned, hoping that we could save the day . . ." he seemed like he was quitting after having seen his friends suffering and disappearing one after another before his eyes.

"No! We returned because someone should put an end to all this. I am going to see what exists over there, in the stinky room. Maybe I can find something functional to help him break those chains." Angelina went close with the flashlight in her hand to take a look. She looked into the room, between the spaces the steel bars on the window were creating. Turning the flashlight onto it she was flabbergasted and her eyes stared dreadfully on that grotesque show. That room was filled with human skeletons and bones. She lighted deeper into the room, but it seemed a huge one. The beam couldn't reach the far wall. As far as she could she, the floor had bodies all over and also stuffs such as clothes, bags, glasses and etc. Its use, an obvious one; keeping prisoners, squeezing the life out of them.

"Oh my god . . ." she whispered.

"What is it? What do you see?"

"It's full of dead persons in there!"

"NO!" Zik went close to have a look too. That moment, something happened to Tiger. He started shaking and his eyes went white. The pupils of his eyes had turned backwards and he was moving his lips as a person who wants to talk but can't use his voice. Zik and Angelina forgot for the moment about the room and run to help him.

"Tiger, Tiger! What is happening? Talk to me man?" Zik was trying to bring him back in his senses. Talking to him, slapping him, nothing seemed to work. Angelina was watching him unable doing anything. Some seconds passed, while both trying to figure out what to do so shall they not lose him and the shaking stopped. The pupils of his eyes went back to their original position and everything looked as if it had turned back to normal. Tiger opened his eyes little by little until he saw Zik looking at him apprehensively. He took some deep breaths until he drew his self together.

"What happened? What was that Tiger? Did the spirit made this to you?" Zik couldn't stop worrying about his near dead friend.

"I am fine . . ." Tiger responded.

"That didn't look fine to me at all . . ." Angelina in sequence added.

"I had a vision, just now . . ." and he was still trying to recover his senses, eating his words.

"What was it about? Can you tell us?" Zik didn't want him to further talk if he couldn't do it.

"I know what happened here, approximately eighty years ago!" That statement of his, made them watching him with their ears wide open. They were ready to learn everything about it and on top of it, how it ended back then. Tiger coughed a couple of times; Zik asked him whether he was feeling able to talk, considering his current state. He was affirmative; he needed a second to forget about the headache and to put his thoughts on a sequel.

"Adam Black knew about the spirit as you remember and he talked to Lewis when he found out about his plans . . ."

"That's where the diary stopped." Angelina said.

"Correct. It had a reason why he stopped writing after that day. Once Lewis learned that the spirit had evil intentions, he and Adam agreed to search any possible way of how stopping it. Ahead of it, Lewis talked to his family. He said to his wife Jessica, that she should take Felicia and leave the village. He didn't want to tell her more so as not to scare her. He just told her that there has been a crisis and it would be better if she and his daughter were out of town. She wanted to know more but Lewis told her that it was for their own safety not to know anything further and pleaded her to leave the village immediately. Jessica suspected that something was going on, something that had to do with the spirit, but she didn't say anything and in a few hours she had packed the essentials and she had left. She went to the closest town to stay in an old aunty which she had there. She asked her auntie to take care of Felicia and she told her that she had to go back at Haurr because she had forgotten something of a great importance. She lied that time, she was going back to learn the truth and what was going on, now that her daughter was safe. In the meanwhile, Lewis and Adam have been at the library, searching inside the book with title Haurr, anything that could help them stop the spirit. Inside the pages, everything was written. It was saying about Lewis's life before meeting the spirit and it had every detail, as why he was ideal for a deal as the one he had committed. Lewis was fulfilling all the conditions that the spirit needed in order to come back to life. It was also including inside what the spirit was. Lewis remained expressionless. He couldn't believe that the being he thought that had saved his life, was a creature from another world, which had died and it had found a way through that contact to come back to life once again. After having this knowledge, Lewis wanted to stop it at any cost. Unfortunately, they found that cost. After some sort of details about the deal, there was the way to cancel it. Main solution was that the spirit had to die but it wasn't that easy. They had to sacrifice a pure soul which was residing in a drained body. Paying the cost would be a total inversion. Everything that had happened from the time the deal had been contacted till then would have been erased. That meant of course, that Lewis will lose everything, not only material things but also his wife and child. The time would be the same as it was, but things would be different as the wish would have never had happened. He read again and again if there was another way, but there was none. In the end he had to choose whether he would sacrifice the entire village and the spirit would return or him, losing the love of his life and his only daughter forever. It was a tough decision to take. Adam saw that Lewis was desperate and not able choosing the one or the other, he advised him one thing. If he really wanted to save his family, that was the only way, and who knows, maybe the future for him, would be to be together with Jessica eventually. Saying those words, Adam gave courage to Lewis and alleviated his thoughts. But that wasn't the only problem that they had.

Lewis didn't know what the book was meaning when it was saying, someone with a pure soul and a drained body. Making that reference, Adam told him that it was talking about someone who was being sick and had committed no murder most likely. Adam had read somewhere, that the human soul in order to stop being pure, should do several actions, that the humans where doing more or less during their life time. But the one with the most highly sin action above all, where to kill. He explained him that if someone kills somebody else, changes, becomes different than what was used to be. The soul's body is stigmatized forever. Thus he suspected that they needed at least someone who had not committed a murder in his entire life. The drained body, it was easier, they needed only someone who was sick. Adam was seeing too sure about everything, so they decided to proceed in the extermination of the spirit once and for all. Lewis was hoping that he was right but he had no other solution than to believe Adam's conclusions.

They knew now how to kill it and what the cost was, but who would be making the sacrifice? Adam took that responsibility on his shoulders. He explained him that since he had cancer and his was too old already, he wanted to end his life by doing something poetic and not let himself die without honor. At first, Lewis had some objections but Adam insisted and at the end he made him agree. They planned everything that evening and they were ready to take action at this same night. The sooner the better they said." Tiger coughed some times and took a deep breath. Zik gave him some short of hits on his back to help me get through with the cough.

"Where was I? Oh yeah, I remembered. That night, they have planned everything, beginning about how to lure the spirit, ending about how to do the ritual to kill it. Lucky for them, the book was giving precise descriptions, how to cancel the deal by doing the sacrifice. Sadly, that night, Jessica returned at the mansion contingency. She walked through the hall and she went at the kitchen to check. None of the working stuff was there. She started looking at the first floor and she realized that the mansion either was empty or everyone was upstairs. She supposed that everyone has gathered in the first floor. Having that though, she went to the up floor. Inside the ball room, the two men had set up their trap. They had made a circle made by symbols on the floor with Lewis blood, which was essential for the ritual, and they had covered it with a carpet. Inside the circle, Adam who was supposedly bound, wasn't. They have though making the spirit believe that Lewis was on spirit's side and that he was ready to sacrifice anyone in order to be with the spirit. Everything was perfect. The right time, Adam would be unbound himself, grabbing the spirit and Lewis will both shooting them with a gun. I forgot to mention that they had found a way not only to cancel the deal but to kill it as well. Adam had noticed from his research that the spirit was intangible but not always. If it was coming in contact with a living body, that of a human, he was losing this ability. Knowing that, the plan they have come up with, seemed perfect.

Nevertheless they didn't count Jessica's sudden return. The spirit was in the ball room. Lewis was explaining to it everything he had heard and mentioned that he wanted to be with it forever because he had found intriguing that the spirit was so powerful. He told it, that he was willing to sacrifice his own friend, in order to prove to it that he was on its side. Adam was in the center of the room, bounded on the chair, the spirit was standing already inside the circle they have made but it was covered up by the carpet. Lewis was out of the circle and was talking to the spirit from distance since he didn't want to come into the circle and destroy perhaps the ritual. The spirit was cutting rides around Adam. Soon it had to be the right time to do it. However, when Lewis was explaining at the spirit that he was willing do anything, his wife who was standing at the door, have heard everything and made an appearance at that time. She was disappointed and she was yelling at Lewis who didn't know why she was there at that moment. He tried to calm her down, but of course Jessica after having heard all that, couldn't stop blaming him cause he had deceived her. The spirit commanded Lewis to kill his wife instead of his friend because she already knew a lot. Lewis froze before that command.

The spirit realized that something wrong was going on and it turned his eyes on Lewis and attacked him. Jessica saw the spirit coming and stood on the way to stop it. The spirit raised its hand and it was ready to hit her and then a shot fire sounded. Lewis shot the spirit but the bullet passed through it of course. Jessica couldn't understand what was going on but it was too late for her. She already had her throat cut from the spirits hand. Crying and tears came from Lewis's eyes and throat. That very moment, Adam run through the spirit and grabbed it from behind, he yelled at Lewis to shoot them. Lewis had his eyes covered on tears and couldn't aim right, but eventually he did. He shot the spirit right in his heart and the same bullet, passed right through Adam. The ritual was complete. Adams blood had been spread on the floor. The spirit, shocked that they have managed to hurt it, was looking at his bleeding wound. Adam felt at the floor having a smile on his face at the same time as he was looking the spirit vanishing. Its body was turning into dust and at the last second looked at Lewis and made an angry face."

"That's all that you saw? This doesn't explain why the spirit is back after having died once . . . damn!!!" Zik disappointed said.

"Zik . . . You should better come over here . . ."

"What is it? Tiger give me a second my friend and I'll be right back at you." Zik told him kindly and Tiger seemed to have no problem with that.

Angelina, before the end of the story, was walking searching the room and she was standing at the door with the caged window. She was seemed worried about the content of the room at the other side. Angelina went close with the flashlight in her hand to take a look. She looked into the room, between the spaces the steel bars on the window were creating. Turning the flashlight onto it she was flabbergasted and her eyes stared dreadfully on that grotesque show.

"Oh my god . . ." she whispered.

"What is it? What do you see?"

"It's full of dead persons in there!"

"NO!" Zik went close to have a look too. She stepped aside so he had a view of whatever was in there whilst he was coming closer. Angelina for one more time lighted the room. What was located in there was terrible and could definitely explain the terrible and also unbearable smell.

Ω

Tones of human bodies were behind that door. That room looked like a mausoleum and the smell was clearly because of all those dead bodies in there. That room was filled with human skeletons and bones. She lighted deeper into the room, but it seemed a huge one. The beam couldn't reach the far wall. As far as they could see, the floor had bodies all over and also stuffs such as clothes, bags, glasses and etc. It's use, an obvious one; keeping prisoners squeezing the life out of them.

Zik was trying to believe that this was not real but it was unfortunately the ugly truth. He had experienced things that were knick-knacks. But this was out of his imagination. The entire village had to be buried over there and to top if off, he recognized two of the dead bodies. Aprilia's and Mark's were there among the stack. He asked from Angelina to light up further down and he also saw Kathrin's body, just few meters away from the rest of his friends. He knew now that his friends were absolutely dead and most probably there was nothing to do to save them. That time, a thought passed through his mind. A though so dark as the mausoleum he was looking at.

If the spirit, was a spirit which it could grant wishes, he could have asked it to redone what's done. But no, that would be a big mistake, having a deal with that . . . thing. That though, as fast as it passed through his mind, the same way it went away too. Angelina saw her dead friends too and she put her hands in front of her mouth. She started crying and she gave the flash light to Zik. She couldn't bear anymore the sight of that terrible place.

"What is in there? Why are you crying Angelina? Zik what is there?" Tiger wanted to get an answer.

"This . . . How did all this happen? Why that thing is still alive? How does the story ends!?" Zik was having all those questions. He was feeling that for each answer he was having, more questions were on the cards. Like he was part of a big, continuing and unstoppable puzzling game.

"WHAT LIES BEHIND THE DOOR?" Tiger screamed this time and both Angelina and Zik came again back to the reality. Angelina first took the courage to inform him. He had to know the truth after all.

"Tiger . . . I'm so sorry . . . I don't think that our friends are still alive?" and she gave him to understand that behind that room, the corpses of their beloved friends were.

"No way . . . fuck . . ." Tiger started crying too. The atmosphere presently among them was blue. Zik had put his back at the door and he was sitting on the floor. Angelina was comforting Tiger but she was crying as well. The tears on Zik's eyes didn't last long. With a fast move, he stood up and he was shining.

"I know!" he gladly yelled.

"What do you know?" Angelina asked and she cleared some of her tears.

"The spirit is still alive, that means that something didn't go well by killing it. Right?"

"Most probably" Angelina answered back.

"That means that if we kill the spirit. If we really kill the spirit, everything will undo. Maybe we will go years back but if Lewis never had made the deal, then we would never been here too!" What Zik was saying, it had logic, which was bringing hope back on the table.

"Release me! Find a way to release me now! I will finish what I started!" Tiger had regained his spirit again. He was moving and straggling to release himself from those uncommon chains that where holding him. If he could undo what happened those days, he was willing to even give his life for it. Angelina tried one more time to release him but it was pointless. The chains most probably would be able to be unlocked by the spirit and only. Tiger was dying and he saw that there was no way for him to be released.

"You should better go. Being here it makes no sense right now. Stefan may be in danger at the moment. The spirit didn't come after you, so that means that it is heading to them" Zik looked Angelina and they realized that he was right. The spirit wasn't there, and if it wasn't there that means that he could be only to one place, at the living room to get Stefan and sick Melody.

"What about you Tiger? We can't just leave you here to suffer!" Angelina said.

"Don't bother about me. I am going to die even if we made it to the closest town. Just find the spirit, kill it and undo the spell. There is no other way. Even if we survive, what are we going to tell to their parents?" Tiger was absolutely right in everything. Zik and Angelina they gave the greatest of all weapons with their hint, hope. That it was enough for him. He closed his eyes and he fainted. Now the two of them, were having the necessary knowledge of stopping it. They still needed a sick person to do the ritual.

"I am not sick. Neither do you, right my heart?"

"No Zik, if I were I would have told you. So, who is it to get sacrificed?" Both mind, went at Melody and a terrible though passed from their minds. First of all, they had to sacrifice her but this wasn't the main reason why they stood looking at the empty corridor. The spirit most probably had already noticed that there was someone with a sickness and that one was Melody. Having done this mistake in the past, it didn't want to repeat it. That's what passed through their minds. The spirit was after Melody that's why it hadn't showed up at them. Once they realized that, they started running to the living room leaving Tiger behind them bleeding and losing his life with each second which was passing.

"I think that is after Melody!" Zik said while both running.

"I had the same though. It wants to stop anything that can kill it before it happens." Angelina told Zik and she passed the wine collection which was stored in that place. They were doing their best, with the strength they had left, to go back and kill the spirit. But they couldn't go like that. In any case, they needed a plan of action. They were still running and they were almost out of the cellar.

"You know . . . At first we need a plan, don't you think babe?" Zik told Angelina while still running.

"I agree. What do you suggest?" Angelina stopped putting this crucial question on the table.

"I don't have a plan . . . But we will need to recreate the circle with the symbols, if we want it dead and to lure it inside it. Correct?"

"Correct. Does that mean that we have to go back at the library to get that book? And which one it was? The library was full of those books that had the same title. I don't think that the spirit wants the book to be found."

"Not necessarily. We can use the once already used one which Adam and Lewis draw that day. I'm guessing that it will still be there!"

"True! Now we need to check it for sure and we also need a plan."

"I have something in mind; the problem is that must we really need to sacrifice Melody? That is the only think I'm holding back for this."

"I know. It's hard but even if Melody dies now, everything will be rewritten and all of us will be alive. So we don't need to worry!" she gave him a kiss and saw him her compassion. After that, they continued running. They run all the way upstairs until the dancing room. The door was unlocked obviously and first thing to do was to check under the red thick but beautifully handmade carpet, if the ritual symbol was still under there. The carpet wasn't covering all the floor of that big room luckily, but only a part of it in the middle. Not a small one, but it was possible to move it aside and have a look under it. So they did. Both together, got one side of the carpet and started moving it aside. Their suspicions were right. The symbol was still there. No one had messed with it. It looked in a perfect condition. With a fast move, they put the carpet back to look exactly how it used to look like and having now no doubt they proceed to the execution of the plan.

"The plan is simple. What I have in mind, is to go downstairs and find a way to mislead the spirit away from them, if of course they are not dead yet. I don't want to think if something bad had already happen at them."

"Continue . . ." Angelina urged him.

"Of course, I'm sorry. I will mislead it in here. Meanwhile, inform them about our plans and what has to happen in order to make everything as it used to be plus putting an end on this. I will run as fast as I can to make it until here and try to follow the soonest possible. When everyone will be in the room, I'll let the spirit take Melody and that's where I will kill it.

"What do you mean? The spirit needs to be touched by someone in order to do not be intangible. Not to touch someone and it top of it how are you going to kill it?"

"I am well conserved of the touching part. What I meant was that once you will come into the room, we will let the spirit take Melody and she will be the one touching it. The spirit will think that it took her but that will work for us. That precisely moment, Melody has to touch it and I'll stab it. I still have the knife that I took from the kitchen, remember?" and he took it off from his back, where he was keeping in on his pant belt.

"Do you think that this is going to work?" Angelina told him and sounded somehow pessimist about his plan. Zik didn't know himself if the plan would work. But at the moment he couldn't come up with something better. They had to give a shot fast as they were running out of time. Having agreed that they will follow that plan they went out of the room and running again, passed all the rooms in the second floor and stood before the staircase.

"We have to do this my life. Are you ready?" Angelina told Zik and holed his hand. Zik nodded and took a big breath. They were afraid, not scared about the spirit but about what was to happen if the plan wouldn't work. However, there was any longer another option. They had to be optimistic and shall not have any fear to continue what they have started. They arrived at the living room but they couldn't hear anything. They thought that their friends had been already taken by it. Horror painted in their faces and they went fast near the fire place where they had let them. To their big surprise, Stefan was sleeping with Melody in his arms. Angelina smiled that moment; she found the scene very cute.

"They seem fine to me" she said.

"But this has to make you wonder, where is it?" Behind Zik, a shadow appeared on the roof. A shadow, not other than this of the spirit. It was visible because of the fireplaces light and it was growing and growing while it was coming closer to them. The flames on the fireplace began fainting and eventually disappeared completely.

Darkness has fallen once again and this time, not at a good moment. Angelina switched on the flashlight or at least she tried to. It didn't work.

"Shit, I can't switch it on. I think that the batteries went off." She complained.

"I don't know if it's the batteries or its doing . . . Nevertheless, we can still see a bit because of the lightings. Stefan, Melody! Wake up, we have a situation here." That unforeseen circumstance, it may have to change their plan. Without light, it wouldn't be easy for any of them to make it upstairs.

Stefan opened his eyes and yawned making some stretching using his hands. Melody woke up too looking around, trying to figure out what exactly was happening. They saw whenever they could, Zik and Angelina being in guard. It didn't take them long, to understand that the spirit was in the room.

"Good, you are awake now. We have a situation." Zik told them.

"What is going on?" Stefan made the question but didn't have time to wait for an answer. Something grabbed his hand and it wasn't Melody. Stefan was found to suspend on the air like something was having him caught by his hand. Behind him a shadow appeared after the strike of lighting. It was the spirit in its true form. Stefan was surprised at first but he took control of the situation. He swung and moving his arms around. He hit the spirit on its face and made it release him. He felt on the floor but stood without falling down. All four came close to each other, creating a single mass. The spirit screamed and the sound of its scream made them cover their ears. It did it once and then it stopped. They could see it, not clearly but they could see it. It was standing there, next to the sofa.

"We have a plan but we don't know how to complete it without light." Zik whispered at Stefan's ear.

"What for a plan? We need a plan as soon as possible"

"We have found a way to stop it. But to do that, Melody has to . . ." and he changed his voice tone making it sound more companionable.

"Get sacrificed in the dancing room."

"What?" Melody said astounded, listening to their little talk.

"Don't be afraid. If we kill it, everything is going to be as it used to be. You will not stay dead forever. This is our only alternative now. After all we have nothing to lose but to earn."

"Why . . ." Stefan was about to ask something but the spirit start walking up to them. Breathing out loud and making slow but heavy steps, eventually stood before them. They were afraid and they didn't want to separate since they couldn't see where to go. Being all together at least, would make them feel better. There was no other resonance apart from the storm outside. The spirit was looking at them and they were looking at the spirit. Zik felt like he had something to say but there was no point. He knew that now, it was the end for them too. Without light to see where to go, and having that thing in front of them, the only solution they had was to wait for their deaths or to pray for a miracle. The spirit smiled and stretched its hand to catch someone. Then a tiny sound heard and the lights of the mansion went on. The spirit went into surprise and started looking around, wondering how did that happened.

"Now is our chance Zik! Guys, let us go to the dancing room!" Angelina screamed and they all start running to that direction. The spirit saw them running and began running behind them. It was faster than they were. Stefan was trying to hold Melody, but she was too sick to run as it needed.

"Take her with you. Save her . . . save us. I'll stay" He said and went in front of Melody and stood on the spirit's way.

"Stefan, No!!!!" Melody screamed and started crying. Zik took her hand and told her that everything is going to be fine, but they just had to go now. The spirit stopped when Stefan stretched his arms and saw to it that he had to pass through him. They continue running, having Melody crying for Stefan and she couldn't take her eyes off him. The last picture see could caught, was the spirit driving its hand aiming his chest.

"Here we go finally . . ." Stefan said and closed his eyes having a smile of relief written in his face.

"Next time, I'll try to live. I swear. Guys, save my Melody." He said to himself and he felt the full arm of the spirit piercing right through his chest. He spill out a lot of blood, the spirit took off his hand and Stefan meet its eyes. The spirit seemed truly pleased for what it had prospered. Stefan first kneeled and then he lay on the floor.

Ω

Stefan's body was on the floor with a big hole passing right through his chest. The blood around him was creating a small lake expanding slowly, really slowly, like the stain when a glass full of water brakes.

"NOOOOOO!!! Melody screamed and braked a shutting. Zik couldn't see what had happened. He just pulled her hand in order to follow him and Angelina, who they were heading upstairs as fast as they could. After a second they had fully gone.

"*Those fouls, they think that they can kill me, but they did a serious mistake boy. I heard about their plan. Do you know why they wanted your girlfriend to get sacrificed? Because they thought that she has what it takes to take me down. Unfortunately, they were wrong. You were the one that had to be sacrificed. Now, I am going to kill each and every one of them and with no one else being able to stand on my way, I'll live again!*" The spirit was talking to the near dead Stefan. It had a monstrous voice, deep and wild but still the feeling of pleasure which it had, was printed on his voice. It had won and it wanted to make this victory of its sweeter by telling Stefan that they have failed.

Stefan when he heard that, he widely opened his eyes and left watching the empty hall. The spirit was walking sluggishly, taking his time doing heavy steps, making a grave sound as it was stepping to each one of the staircases, leading up. In the intervening time, Melody, Zik and Angelina entered the dancing room. The lights were giving the room a gorgeous wealth of magnificence. But there was neither time nor mood for them to dazzle the splendid room. They had to be prepared to kill the spirit. Melody after having dragged, despite her will, in there, aggressively pulled her hand off Zik.

"What do you think you are doing? Stefan is dead and we did nothing to help him! He was there and you let him die. You want to call yourselves "friends" "she said as she was crying deeply. Zik did to talk to her but Angelina stopped him and gave him a stern look to understand that she was the one who had to talk to her.

"Melody, listen carefully. I know what you think right now . . ." Melody interrupted her before she started her speech.

"You have no idea what Stefan meant to me? You don't know a thing Angelina!!! All these years, I was by his side, trying to give him hope to live, to do not die. And in an instant, all those years went lost for no reason. It wasn't supposed to happen now and not in this terrible way." And she continued crying.

"What do you mean . . . ?" Angelina got jumbled and had no idea what she was talking about.

"Stefan was sick, ok!? He had cancer. Why do you think he was always this calm and was doing whatever he liked? He didn't know when he was going to die. The doctors didn't know when it could happen. Maybe 2 years from now, maybe 10. It was a first seeing case. He didn't suppose to die like this . . ." and she was trying to calm herself down but it was hopeless. Angelina, meet her eyes with Zik's. A though passed before both eyes. They realized that the one, who had to die, was not Melody but Stefan. They were seeking for that kind of disease or sickness, a systemic disease that is inside your body and leads unavoidably, like Adams. Melody was only having flue at the time. Stefan had the real weak body that the ritual needed. However, they realize it a bit late. In the entrance of the room, under all those dazzling lights, the spirit appeared. It was moving slowly, taking his time now directing at the center where they were.

"What happens now? Even if Melody got sacrificed, the spirit will not die? What's the plan now Zik?" Angelina was asking Zik fretfulness. The spirit was coming all the more closer to them and they didn't know what to do. Zik wasn't talking, he was just standing there. Speechless as the spirit was coming on him.

"ZIK! WAKE UP! We have to figure something out! It can't end like this!" Angelina was shouting on him waiting for a response, but this wasn't happening. Melody she was on the floor now, looking at the spirit, prisoner of the fear not able to do something too. Bewildered as she was, she began running. But she didn't start running to an exit but to the spirit which was only few meters away from them. She passed next to Zik and stood before the spirit.

"I have a wish that I want you to fulfill!" she demanded. The spirit showed no interest in her proposal but it stopped exact in front of her.

"I know that you can hear me and I know that you can understand me. I want to make a deal with you!" she said again with more zealous than before.

"Why shall I ever do a deal with you? I am on my way to come back to life once I kill all of you. But more than that, you don't meet the standards." The spirit rejoined, with his tremendous voice. Angelina was biting her lips and started crying, having no more ideas of how to make everything as it was before.

"PLEASE!!!" she screamed.

"Please, make everything as it was before and I will do whatever you want!" Angelina was begging the spirit with tears in her eyes, to give her a wish, a second chance to make everything as it used to be before they step a foot on the village. The spirit was looking at her for some seconds and then it gave her a smile; it was a creepy and sinister one, and it did a step forward. It was face to face with Angelina right now and she was still waiting for an answer. She wasn't afraid at all, she was holding every hope that she could bring her friend back and not only. She also wanted to keep the promise which she has given to Felicia. She was willing to do anything, in order to stop it or to make things normal again. The spirit enlarged his smiled and it was obvious now that it was ready to do something violent. Angelina had no time to react now; it was too close to her.

"Angelina, touch it! Do it now!" Zik yelled, as he was running holding the knife on his hands. Angelina gave him a quick look and then she did as Zik said. She jumped into the spirit and caught it. The spirit got ad hoc, being dazed by her sudden action. Angelina was holding it as hard as she could without giving it a chance to escape. Zik run into it and at the same time Angelina was holding its leg, he screamed. All the pain, hate and anger that he was feeling at the present, went out with that scream.

"AAAAAAA!!!" and he stabbed the spirit right on the center of its chest. It was a success hit. He felt the knife, going through the spirits skin and penetrating deeper on his flesh. They could do it; they could still kill it before it kills them. The knife was supposed to go all in but it stopped somewhere in the middle. Zik was pushing it to go deeper but nothing was happening. It seemed like it had found a hard part and it couldn't break through it.

Then he looked at the spirits face and he saw that it was angry. It was really angry. It caught the knife and was pushing it out of his body. Zik was trying to fight back but there was no point, Spirit's strength, was beyond his power. Eventually, it took it all out and Zik left it from his hands. It threw it away, outside of the room. It caught right after that, Zik's head and it lifted him on the air.

"NO NO NO!!!" Angelina began screaming and she was hitting his leg as hard as she could. The spirit looked at her. At first it threw Zik and its enormous power, made him fly until the center of the room. He felt down and the fall made him scream out of pain. Then he looked at Angelina, she left its leg and it immediately kicked her. She had the same fate as Zik. He kick was extremely strong and she flew close to Zik. She also got a heavy injury cause of the fall and she screamed as well. They were both laying down now and the spirit was mad.

Melody was watching everything, some steps away from the door. The spirit didn't even give her a look. It was going to finish the couple that tried to damage it. Every step it was making, the closer they were coming to death. There was no way out now and no power for them to fight back. During the time they were in pain, laying down on the floor, Zik stopped screaming and start looking at his girlfriend. He remembered all the good times he had with her. How he met her, and the first kiss they had. For him, she was the perfect girlfriend and he was willing to spend all his life next to her. Tears came out of his eyes and Angelina noticed that he had stopped screaming and now he was crying. She slowly, stopped screaming too and she stayed, watching at her boyfriend.

"I love you Angelina, my angel. Since the first time I saw you, I wanted to be with you until the end. I couldn't imagine that it would be so soon. It's a shame . . . I wanted to do so many things with you." Hearing those words, Angelina started having tears on her eyes. Those tears where different that the ones she had before. Those were tears of love and compassion. She was moved by Zik's speech.

"I love you my Love." She said too and she tried to crawl near him. She was crawling on the floor to get near him as it was impossible for her to stand on her feet. She raised her hand, in a desperate attempt to catch his hand. He raised it too, not being able to move, waiting for her to reach him giving her his hand. They were really close, almost there! But as close as they were, so close the spirit was too. It stretched both of his arms and before they made it, it raised them from their necks, in the air.

It was really pissed but was still enjoying this. The last moments of someone before he dies, were for the spirit a way of entertainment and a moment of pure bliss. They could hardly breathe as it was squeezing them all the more harder. They were still trying to help themselves; by holding and pushing with the remaining power it had left inside them its arms, in a failed attempt to escape.

"This is useless, you aren't going anywhere. I will show you what I am capable of. I shall materialize your greatest fear and I will put you into an internal nightmare that you will never be able to escape! As for your girlfriend and the other girl, I am going to eat them and that's how this is going to END! You did a big mistake coming back,

to fight ME!" The spirit said and it was about to give an end to their life's.

This is where something which no one could expect happened. A knife, the same knife that Zik had used in an attempt to kill it, and the spirit had threw out of the room, pierced right through his throat. The spirit split out a dark liquid thing and released them from its hands. It tried to turn into darkness again but it couldn't. Zik and Angelina where on the floor coughing but they were also surprised with what had happened. They couldn't see who had stabbed it. The huge body of the spirit was blocking the one behind it. It slowly turned as it could its head to see who had dared to stabbed it like that.

Stefan was behind him, smiling.

"YOU!" the spirit said full of surprise while spiting black liquids out of his mouth.

"HOW DARE YOU AND YOU ARE STILL ALIVE?" It couldn't accept as true that the only person who can actually stopped it, was there, alive. And it just realized that it had done something really stupid. All alone, had driven itself in the middle of the room where under the red carpet, the seal was.

"This is my last action. When you told me that only I was able to stop you, I just couldn't left myself die. I had to stop you." He gloriously said and turned his eyes on Melody.

"My life, I love you. Next time, let us do it better. Ok?" He said and for one last time he smiled. This was his last smile. He felt down on the floor, contented for his accomplishment. Tears came out from Melody's eyes but this time, a smile was painted on her face.

"Stefan?"Zik enquired behind the spirit, to see if he truly was him. He didn't get any answer and the same time a light appeared. That light was coming out from the spirit's throat. The spirit couldn't believe its eyes; it touched its throat and tried to cover with its hands the hole. But then the light became brighter and was flowing from all its body.

"*No No No!!! This cannot be happening.*"

"He did it. Stefan killed it!" Angelina said surprised and both her and Zik her happy.

"*You low life insects. I . . . I . . .*" Those were its last words. The light became brighter and the spirit exploded leaving only bright pieces suspended on the air. The explosion had them close their eyes and then they opened them again once it ended.

"Zik . . ." Angelina said whereas she was looking at him.

"What is it?" He answered.

"Your body . . ." she told him, showing him that his body had started lighting.

"Your body too" he said and pointed at her. They were both glowing, or better tell, all three were glowing.

"What is happening?" Melody asked, watching with surprise on their friends' bodies and hers, that peaceful light coming out from them.

"*You did it. Thank you.*" A voice heard from somewhere. They looked around and they saw someone standing few meters away from Melody. A bright man, illuminated also by lights, began talking to them.

"*My name is Lewis, Lewis Anderson. I am grateful that you broke the deal I have made almost seventy years ago. I am the one who revealed the secret rooms for you to find Adams notes and I am also the one who turned on the lights. I needed your help to end this and I had to help you. Responsible for your friend's visions, would be me as well. I really, deeply thank you for everything. Time to do things right this time, isn't it?*" He said and disappeared of their sight like a peaceful smoke. That wholehearted light they were feeling made them take a big breath all together and close their eyes. This emotional state was feeling so calm and light and all the room was bursting with light . . .

Ω

It is dark outside 4am in the morning the sun has not yet come out. It's a quiet night and there is not a single resonance in the air to disturb this amazingly peaceful night. There is total darkness in the sky except the lights on the street. It's a summer's night in England and more specific in a house, near the Oxford University. It is not a cold night but not a warm one either. There is a couple, sleeping in a bed and one of them, is opening his eyes. The boy, who was sleeping before in this peaceful night, now is awake.

"Angelina . . . Angelina my love?" he sits on the bed and he is pushing her to wake up.

"Mmmm . . . What is it Zik? What do you want? Let me sleep." She says and she continues trying to sleep.

"Do you remember any of this or is just me?"

"To remember what my love? You had a dream?" she says and she opens her eyes, shitting along with him on the edge of the bed.

"You don't remember any of these? About Haurr?"

"What is Haurr? My love, you probably had a strong dream. Do you want to talk about it later? I want to sleep my love"

"Yes, it's ok. There is nothing to talk about it anyway. Everything is fine, really. Sorry that I woke you up." He smiled at her and he kissed her on the forehead. They laid back to sleep again. Angelina slept right after she put her head back on the pillow. But Zik, stayed awake. He was smiling and he was really happy, because not only they have saved many lives, but also because his friends most probably, wouldn't remember any of these horrible things that had happened to them. He closed his eyes after some minutes and he was feeling glorious. New memories have been added on his mind. This time, almost seventy years ago, Lewis had never done this deal. He saved his own life and he deeply regret it that he tried to suicide. He also as Zik, had the memories from what have happened and he tried to live his life as normal as he could by using his own strength. He tried his best and he succeeded on creating a really nice family and on having an as it should be job. Felicia was close with Zik's family and they had a grandson grandmother relationship. Everything has been done well. He slept for a long time that night.

Next morning, he invited all his friends out, to have dinner all together. They were all there, Stefan, Melody, Tiger, Aprilia, Mark and Kathrin. They had a great night and Stefan, that night was different. He was participating in the conversations and he was more active than he used to be. Something had changed inside him and even if he was dying, he was an entirely different person. A person full of will for life. Melody was seemed happier but she was shy as always. Save for that didn't stopped her for smiling more, as she was having a mentally healthier person by her side. Zik was watching every single one of them, doing his things and continuing dealing with his life. He was enjoying that night and he was extremely happy, that there has been a happy ending in this story. For a second, a thought passed right through his mind. This thought, made him froze and all of a sudden he stopped laughing.

"Oh . . . No . . ." He said . . . frozen there, eyeing terrified . . .